Birthright

A Nobleman Novel

Ronda L. Caudill, Ph.D.

Birthright. Copyright © 2012 by Ronda L. Caudill, Ph.D.

ISBN-13: 978-0-9850179-1-0

ISBN-10: 0985017910

Cover photography by Travis Helton

First edition January 2012. Second edition April 2014.

This book is dedicated to my wonderful husband, Ricky, who has always supported and loved me no matter what. It is also dedicated to my two loving daughters, Brittany and Nikita, who inspire me every day. And to Travis—for technical support. Thank you all. I love you very much.

Birthright

Chapter 1

𝔑ila's skin was moist with a glistening sweet mixture of dewdrops and sweat. Her body was hot and aching under the touch of his fingertips as they caressed her cheek and then lightly glided down the side of her neck and finally gently stroked her skin just atop her bodice. Nila loved how the early morning light caught the beautiful, blue hues in her nobleman's eyes. His marvelous eyes were heavy with lust. The onyx waves of his hair tickled her cleavage as he leaned over her for another kiss—long and deep. Nila felt as though she could drink his essence into her and as if he could do the same at any moment. His hard lean body pressed against her fragile petite flesh. Just when Nila thought that she could no longer breathe, euphoric from the touch of her nobleman's lips, he pulled back, leaving her longing for so much more.

In the distance through the forest they heard the familiar sounds of men, horses, and dogs. Aware that they were forbidden to be together, Nila would risk her life for just one touch of his gentle hands. Risk her life may just be what she was doing, she thought to herself as she heard the galloping horses and barking dogs drawing nearer. They grabbed the few clothes that they had shed. The dogs were closing in fast. There would be no time to escape. Nila was frantic with fear. What would become of them if they were found together? Out of the thicket a soldier lunged at her nobleman with sword drawn.

Then it happened again. She was being pulled away from him back to another reality. She desperately reached out to him but could not hold her ground. Nila cried out in despair as she helplessly watched her beautiful, nobleman battle for his life. Their eyes met and held one last gaze before Nila found herself back in her own bed lying in a pool of sweat and desire. She felt the longing for her nobleman tugging at her heart. But it was just another dream—another strange dream in a huge collection of strange dreams that she had been having since the night of her 17th birthday.

Nila had no idea who the beautiful nobleman was. All she knew about him was what he looked like—dressed like a nobleman from the 18th century, wearing clothing of red and purple—and that his touch was unreal. In her dreams, she desperately longed for and loved him. Nila lay there with the moonlight cascading through her open window casting ominous shadows about the room. The tendrils of those shadows reached out from the dark and tugged at her aching heart.

Nila knew that there would be no more sleep that night. She would lie there in an endless state of abyss and obsess over that dream as well as others about the nobleman, as she called him since she had no other name for him. Nila lay there for what seemed like an eternity pondering her dreams but she finally found sleep.

A car horn blasted. *Oh, no! It's Sherry. Damn, she's early.* Nila looked at her clock on the nightstand beside the bed. *Eight o'clock! Crap, I overslept.* Nila grabbed her cell phone from the nightstand and texted, "OMG. Overslept. B down n a sec."

It's the first day of my junior year, and I'm going to school looking like crap. Nila riffled through thrown clothes until she found a white, cotton, mini-skirt with eyelet lace around the hem and a thin, white, cotton, button-up blouse with pink trim. She topped her casual look off with a pair of tan sandals and a small, tan, hemp purse.

She half-assed brushed her teeth and thought to herself as she looked in the mirror. *What the hell am I going to do with my hair and face?* She brushed through her long, black waves and let them fall freely around her shoulders and down her back. It looked like a blue-black, flowing waterfall. She washed her face with clear water followed by a bit of cocoa butter lotion. She loved the way it smelled. She put on some deodorant and gave a small spray of honeysuckle to her neck and wrists. She grabbed her canvas purse and sketchpad. That's all she needed for the day anyway. It was the first day, and they wouldn't do anything.

Nila heard the car horn again as she stuffed her cell phone into her purse and headed down the stairs of her farmhouse. The old, wooden steps creaked all the way down. She passed the mirror of the downstairs bathroom and gave herself one quick glance. *Well, that's not so bad for a rush job. I don't look the worst that I ever have.* She flew out the front door not bothering to lock it. She lived in a small southeastern town called Legacy and everyone knew everyone else, so neither she nor her father or grandmother ever bothered locking the front door. She couldn't remember if the door ever had a key—she had never seen one. For that matter, she really didn't know if anyone in Legacy locked their doors.

"Damn, Nila. What the hell? Are you trying to make us late on our first day?"

"Language. And no, and I'm sorry. I was asleep when you blew the first time," Nila replied in a low voice. She never spoke loudly. Her grandmother always spouted something about a brawling woman being denied entrance into heaven. It kind of stuck because Nila was as quiet as a church mouse most of the time.

"No way, you got to look like this in five minutes? It's not fair. I have been up since six and don't look that good. What's your secret?"

"Yeah, right. I love you, too. You don't have to be so sweet."

"No, really Nila. Anyway, how'd you oversleep on the first day of school? Weird dreams again?"

"How'd you guess?"

"Well, not only did you oversleep, but you got that look about you that I get after a great date with a hot guy. You know the look I'm talking about."

"I really hate going to school looking like this," Nila said.

"Like what? Even on your worst day you're gorgeous. That hair of yours, I've never seen that color before in my life. And you got the prettiest, sea green eyes; you're petite; not a blemish on your face; and perfect pearly whites to boot," Sherry confessed.

"Yeah, right. I'm short and have the boobs of a 12-year-old. And face it, I'm always off somewhere in my own, little world that I have created in my head, so I appear to be oblivious to everything around me. I act like a total dork when someone tries to carry on a conversation with me. Anyway, thanks for the ride. My dad swears he'll fix my tire tonight."

"No prob. I just can't believe that you busted a tire to keep from hitting a cat."

"I love cats. You know how soft-hearted I am when it comes to animals."

"Yeah, yeah, yeah. Now, about the hot dude from your dreams. When you gonna tell me about him? What does he look like? You're keeping him a bit vague," Sherry prompted.

"I-I don't know. I do have some sketches," Nila confessed shyly.

"You been sketching Mr. Hottie dream man?"

"Yeah. I hate to admit it, but he is becoming kind of an obsession. He's all I think about. It's screwy, I know, since he's not real," Nila replied as they pulled into the parking lot of Legacy High.

"Well. We're here. Let me see the sketches before we go in. I can't wait all day. Give me something to dream about," Sherry coaxed.

"Okay," Nila said as she opened her sketchpad.

"Wow! No wonder you can't get any sleep. He is off-the-charts hot," Sherry said with her mouth gaping as she stared at the sketches.

"If you're done drooling over my dream man, can we please go in?" Nila asked as she carefully closed her sketchpad not wanting to bend the pages that held the images of her beautiful nobleman.

Chapter 2

All eyes were on the pair of girls as they walked into school. The guys who were into the beautiful, innocent, schoolgirl look couldn't turn away when Nila walked by. And when her bff Sherry walked by, the guys who were into the punk, trampy look couldn't get enough of her. Sherry decided to wear as little as the dress code would allow. She had on a short, black, mini-skirt; a black, spaghetti-strap top; thigh-high boots; but no purse to match. She never carried a purse. She kept her driver's license in the car, and she loved the look that she got when she pulled her lunch money out of her bra. Her look was completed by tons of dark makeup that covered a beautiful face and short, spiked, hot-pink hair. She was tall and thin. So the pair really looked like the odd couple. People couldn't understand why they were best friends. They were really nothing alike.

Since they were running late, thanks to Nila, they went straight to homeroom. They always had homeroom together. In fact, they always had most of their classes together. It had been that way since Kindergarten. Nila and Sherry stood there greeting familiar faces—some they had seen over the summer and some they had not. Sherry was going on about the party that she had sneaked out to the night before. She had started going out to parties with some of the wild kids at Legacy High. Nila idly listened to Sherry's obscene party story.

Nila had always been an artistic person, quiet and personal. She opted to stay at home with her grandmother and learn things from her that no school could teach, ancient things. Nila was more than content with her way of life.

Nila was in lala land with Sherry babbling in the background when her eyes caught sight of the new guy across the hall. She couldn't believe her eyes; she thought she surely must have been dreaming. He was a dead ringer for her nobleman. He must have been a doppelganger. The only difference between the new guy and her nobleman was their attire. The new guy was dressed in blue jeans, a band T, and black sneakers. His hair, eyes, facial features, and hands were exactly the same as her nobleman's.

Nila felt as though she would surely hit the floor when Sherry elbowed her. "Hey, are you even listening to me?" When Nila didn't respond, Sherry looked in the direction of Nila's gaze. Lo and behold, there was Nila's dream man standing in the flesh. "What the hell? Don't he look just like–"

And before Sherry could get the words out, Nila said, "Yep. Looks just like him. I think I might die right here." Nila couldn't help but stare as the new guy talked to some guys who she and Sherry were friends with. His black hair lay just above his collar as wild waves kissed the side of his face. His eyes were as blue as the ocean, and his face had gentle noble features. His lean, muscular body leaned against the wall with his gentle hands slightly in the top of his jeans pockets. When he smiled, it made Nila's knees go weak and breath grow short. She had the same euphoria she had in her dreams. She knew that her face must be flushed and that everyone must surely know what she was feeling. That longing ache pounded at her heart.

Then the new guy glanced over at Nila, smiled, and nodded. Nila smiled back shyly and franticly from being caught off guard. She was freaking out. Suddenly, the bell rang, and everyone filtered into their homeroom and the classroom across the hall. The new guy walked into the room across the hall as he glanced over his shoulder at Nila, stumbling into her homeroom. Nila found a seat with Sherry.

"Nila, what the hell? This is so freaky! Why don't you dream me up a hottie dream man like that?"

"What? I-I didn't dream him up," Nila responded defensively.

"I'm just kidding. But seriously, girl, did you ever think you guys may have been together in a past life or something? I know you believe in all that kind of stuff."

"I don't know what to think. I'm so flustered and confused. How can I make it through the day? Can I borrow your car and go home? I'll come back and pick you up at three. Please," Nila begged.

"No way! You're staying right here all day. We are going to figure out this enigma together."

First period bell rang. Everyone scattered, heading off to the first class of the first day of junior year. Mrs. Carver, Nila's homeroom teacher, as well as her art teacher, caught her on her way out the door. "Nila, can I speak to you for a minute?"

"Sure," Nila replied, turning toward Mrs. Carver's desk where the plump, middle-aged, art teacher stood.

"I was wondering if you cared to help me after school on some school murals."

"No prob. But I can't do anything today. I rode with Sherry. My car has a flat. I swerved to miss a cat and busted a tire."

"Oh, I see. I hope no one was hurt."

"No, just my tire."

"Well, that's fine. But if you could stay, I could take you home. That is, unless you have other plans," the art teacher said all the while with pleading eyes.

The truth of the matter was that Nila really didn't have any plans. "Sure, I can do that," Nila replied with a smile.

"Thank you, dear. And here. You'll need this," Mrs. Carver insisted while extending her hand with a late pass for Nila's next class, which happened to be her least favorite—biology.

"Thank you," Nila graciously said, accepting the pink slip from the pleasantly round art teacher. Nila turned and headed to biology, taking her time since she had a late pass in hand. She stopped at the girl's room to check herself out. When she had left in such a hurry that morning, she had no idea that her dream guy was going to be in her reality. She knew that she didn't look her best. She was worried about first impressions. Nila looked into the foggy, old mirror that looked like it had been there since the school was built in the fifties. Nila brushed her hair down with her hands, splashed some water on her face, and took a pee. She gave herself one last glance and was very appreciative of her good genes, pretty hair that was typically calm and manageable, and good complexion. Sherry was always telling Nila that she was not natural. Teens aren't supposed to have such a pretty and unblemished complexion.

Nila was still obsessing over the new guy, but she knew she had to get on with her day. As much as she would like to, she could not hang out in the girl's room all day. She left the restroom, still feeling flushed and overwhelmed. Heading toward biology class, she calmed down. Walking through the door of the biology lab, when she picked her foot up to step forward, a sense of panic flooded her body. She almost turned and ran. But she didn't. She sucked it up and went in, handing Mr. Kinly her late pass.

"Nice of you to join us, Miss Jones," the biology teacher said snidely.

The class giggled. Nila was totally humiliated. She looked up to see where Sherry had saved her a seat. Sherry sat in the back of the room at a lab table that only sat three—Sherry sat on one end, the seat in the middle was empty, and the new guy sat on the other end. Nila felt a huge lump grow in her throat. Her stomach churned. She froze in her tracks, trying to center herself with a moment of meditation.

"Miss Jones, would you please take a seat? It shouldn't be hard to choose one since there is only one left and it happens to be right beside your Siamese twin," Mr. Kinly yelled. He was obviously annoyed with Nila's disruption.

Nila pulled herself together and hurried to the seat Sherry had saved for her.

"What the hell?" Nila mouthed at Sherry.

Sherry shrugged her shoulders, leaned in, and whispered, "I was here first. I swear. I'm sorry, old girl, this wasn't my doing."

"Yeah, really. Then who's doing was it?"

Sherry whispered in her quietest of voices, "Really, I was already here. All the other seats were taken. He was the last one through the door. He sat way over there; guess

I'm not his type. Then as luck would have it, the very last seat in the house was yours."

"Okay, fine," Nila snapped.

"Maybe it's fate, you know," Sherry quietly responded defensively.

"Miss Jones, would you like to share anything with the rest of the class? It appears that the conversation you are having with Miss Parker is very important," Mr. Kinly barked. Nila's snapped her head around.

"I was just explaining to Sherry that I didn't need a ride from her after school because Mrs. Carver wants me to stay and help her on the murals," Nila said panicking not knowing what else to say. She sure didn't want to tell the class the truth about their conversation.

Sherry looked puzzled at Nila and then back to Mr. Kinly, smiled, and shook her head in agreement. "Yeah. Nila was just telling me not wait on her after school."

Nila elbowed Sherry in the ribs and gave her a what-the-hell look.

"Well then, can we proceed?" Mr. Kinly spat.

Nila simply shook her head. She was so embarrassed that her face was as red as Mr. Kinly's nose. Mr. Kinly had a slight drinking problem, so his nose was always as red as a pickled beet.

Sherry mouthed quietly, "Sorry," and shrugged her shoulders.

Nila didn't even glance to her left. She did not want to see the empathetic look that she knew must be on the new guy's face, knowing that she was an abject embarrassment to herself. Nila just sat there and nestled into her own little private world, leaving her miserable body behind while it was tortured with a pathetic lesson that a monkey could teach.

Sherry shook Nila back into reality. "Hey, girl, anybody in there?"

"Sorry," Nila apologized as she snapped back to her senses.

"We're taking about 15 minutes to get to know our lab partners and get familiar with the equipment," Sherry explained.

Nila turned to face the new guy, her face only inches from his. She was so thankful for her unblemished skin and the fact that she had washed her face, brushed her teeth, put on deodorant and perfume, and brushed her hair before she barreled out of the house like a bat out of hell.

Just as Nila turned, the new guy reached out his hand to her. "Hi, I'm Blake Billings. I just moved here from Massachusetts.

Wow Blake, Nila thought to herself. *My nobleman has a name. Blake.* "Hi, Blake. My name is Nila Jones. I've lived here in Legacy all my life. And I am totally embarrassed by the first impression that I undoubtedly made," Nila replied as she reached out her hand to take Blake's in a traditional handshake. But much to Nila's surprise, that's not what happened at all. Blake took her hand palm down to his mouth and lightly kissed it. Nila felt tingles run up and down her spine. She felt like she had been taken back in time, like she had experienced this introduction somewhere, some time ago, in some other life.

Blake slowly let go of her hand, almost reluctantly. "Don't worry. You handled Kinly well, even though you totally lied to him."

Nila was so embarrassed. *Had he overheard their conversation?* Then it was like he had read her mind and was answering her unspoken question. "Don't worry. I didn't catch what was said, but it was a bit more heated than merely not needing a ride home," Blake said with a smile.

Sherry pushed Nila aside as she wriggled her way toward Blake. "Hi, I'm Sherry Parker, Nila's bff."

Blake smiled, reached out, and shook Sherry's hand. "Nice to meet you, Sherry."

"So, what brings you to Legacy?" Sherry pried.

"Um, well, my parents' ancestors were originally from here in Legacy. So I thought this would be a fitting place to scatter their ashes. I really liked the place and decided this might be a nice place to settle for a while."

"Your parents' ashes?" Sherry questioned further.

"Yeah, they were killed in an accident. My aunt helped me to become emancipated. She wanted to adopt me, but I wanted to be on my own since I was almost 18 anyway. But I'm going to live with her while she's here in Legacy."

"How long is she staying?" Nila asked.

"Not sure."

The damn bell rang just as Nila was beginning to feel comfortable around Blake Billings, the new guy, her nobleman.

Blake said to Nila, "Thanks for being so hospitable to me. It's hard being the new kid, you know."

"No prob," Nila replied with a smile, thinking he must surely being lying through his teeth, a gorgeous guy like him having any kind of troubles anywhere was beyond comprehension.

"Maybe I'll see you later. At least I hope so," Blake said in a low, gentle but seductive voice.

"Yeah, me too," Nila replied as she picked up her books.

The three headed to the door together, but Nila and Sherry went to the right toward Nila's next-to-her-least favorite class, math. Blake went left. Nila and Sherry walked closely and giggled—awed about the new guy, the dream guy, the nobleman and how he had appeared to enjoy Nila's company.

The two girls reached Nila's class first. "Aren't you glad you stayed?" Sherry smirked as if to say I told you so.

"Yeah, I'm still a little nervous. I can't wrap my head around all this."

"There must be a reason he's here, and you've been dreaming about him, right?"

"I guess."

Sherry pulled Nila in close for a hug, not uncommon for the two best friends. They were more like sisters than best friends. Even though Sherry's outward appearance would indicate a cold and crass person, Nila always felt comforted by Sherry's touch and words. Nila enjoyed the feel of Sherry's cheek against her own, the wonderful way that Sherry always smelled, and just the bond that they had. It was a bond that she knew no other two people in the world had ever shared or ever would share.

"Now don't worry about it. Just enjoy your day," Sherry whispered in Nila's ear as she gave Nila an extra reassuring squeeze.

"Okay, I'll try to," Nila replied as she heard someone yell, "PDA, PDA." She looked up to see Sherry's latest guy in a long string of guys, Kevin.

"Can I join in?" he said as he approached the girls.

"Screw you," Sherry said as she let go of Nila and grabbed Kevin's hand. "Nila, I'll catch you later," Sherry said looking back over her shoulder at Nila as she bounced down the hall arm-in-arm with her latest catch.

"Okay," Nila yelled as she went into trig class.

She hated all math, but she was an honor student and had to take the hard classes. No sooner had she sat down when the bell rang for the next class. "Damn, where'd the time go," she mumbled under her breath. Her seat was at the back of the room, so she was one of the last to get out the door. She would have been concerned about being late for her next class if it wasn't art. Nila knew that Mrs. Carver wouldn't say anything to her.

Nila couldn't wait for art class. It was her refuge, and it helped her get through the rest of the day. There was a table that she always sat at—her table—at the back of the room by a window with a spectacular view of an old maple tree. The tree was one of the oldest maple trees in town. The school had plans to build an addition where the tree was. The tree was going to be cut down. But the historical society had something to say about that. As soon as they caught wind of the school's plans, they intervened, proving that the tree was more than 400 years old, and forced an injunction to protect the tree forever. So there it stood, Nila's muse. Nila felt like the tree communicated with her. Like it had a story to tell her. Like it was whispering some big tale but not loud enough for her to hear it clearly.

No one else wanted the table in the back of the room because it was old and nothing was convenient to it— all of the supplies were on the other side of the room. But this was totally okay with Nila, because she loved her privacy during art class.

But when Nila entered the room and headed toward her table, she was surprised and taken aback. Someone was already sitting at her table. It was Blake Billings. She didn't know what to think or what to do. No one ever sat at that table but her. She had never had to share it before. And to her knowledge, no one in any of the other art classes sat at it either. Nila hesitantly walked to the table and said, "Hey, don't think I'm stalking or anything but I always sit here. I love the view. Do you mind?"

"No, of course not," Blake replied as he started to gather up his things.

"Oh, no! That's not what I meant. I just wanted to make sure that you didn't mind if I sat here, too. I didn't mean that I wanted you to leave," she said feeling totally embarrassed.

"Great. I would much rather sit here with you as to sit anywhere else in the room. Maybe I can get to know you a little better," Blake said with a huge smile.

"Well, I guess you can try."

It was really strange. Nila felt so nervous when she saw Blake from a distance and when she thought about him. But the closer she got to him, the more at ease she felt. When he spoke the first word to her, it felt as if she were being drawn into him completely.

"Class, Class," Mrs. Carver yelled out. Not in the Kinly-type yell but more like a friend trying to get one's attention. Mrs. Carver began to tell them a bit about what they would be doing throughout the year—about a field trip to a local museum, a nature muse field trip as she called it, and the school murals project. Mrs. Carver said, "Today, I want you all to give me a sample of your work. It can be anything of your choice. I will be choosing students to help me with the murals."

Just then, Nila's arch nemesis, Dawn Williams, pranced through the door and threw her late pass on Mrs. Carver's desk. "Well, what an honor, Miss Williams. We are graced with your presence once again this year. Now take a seat, please," Mrs. Carver snapped.

It was so out of character to hear that tone come from Mrs. Carver. She was such a great teacher and got along with almost everyone, everyone that is except Dawn Williams and her family. Dawn's father owned a car dealership in town. They were totally loaded. Dawn thought she was Miss High and Mighty, but basically she was just a royal pain in the ass. She waltzed around in her designer clothes, hand bag, shoes, makeup, hair and nails all done up, and tanned from a summer of leisure. She scoped the room. *Oh crap,* Nila thought to herself as Dawn focused in on the new guy. Nila felt her heart drop and wondered how she could compete with that.

"Anywhere?" Dawn asked as she undressed Blake with her eyes. A huge smile plastered across her face.

"Yes, anywhere. Just sit. Please," Mrs. Carver sighed.

Dawn made a beeline toward Nila and Blake's table. Mrs. Carver glanced around just before Dawn reached her destination. She knew that Dawn and Nila did not get along. It was understood that that was Nila's table. In fact, Mrs. Carver had asked the guidance counselor to put the two girls in separate art classes. But the guidance counselor didn't seem to care about Mrs. Carver's request. And there Dawn was in the same class with Nila, ready to cause problems. Dawn was no artist and didn't even pretend to be. She took the class because there was not a lot of reading but a lot of field trips.

Mrs. Carver immediately halted this disruption in its tracks. "Oh no, Dawn. Not there."

"What? You said anywhere."

"You really need to find a seat in front of me. You know, so I can give you special attention," Mrs. Carver said with a condescending smile.

"Really, Mrs. Carver, I don't need special attention."

"Oh, but I think you do. Here is a nice spot right beside my desk."

Dawn continued to argue about the seating. Nila was holding her breath, hoping against all hope that Mrs. Carver would win this one.

"Dawn Gale Williams, you will take this seat beside my desk or you will march to Mr. Miller's office," Mrs. Carver said through her teeth. No one in the class had ever heard her get that angry before. Nila wasn't sure if anyone in town had ever heard her that angry before.

Mr. Miller was the principal at Legacy High. He was once an army sergeant. He was a very stern man and ran the school like boot camp. But there were usually no problems at Legacy because of Mr. Miller.

However, Mr. Miller had a soft spot for Nila and everyone at school knew it. He had dated Nila's mother, Mary. This was way before Mary married Nila's father, David. Mr. Miller had always loved Mary, but they had wanted different things out of life. They both knew that no matter how much they loved each other, it wouldn't work between them and they would be miserable together. So, Mr. Miller joined the army and left Legacy. When he returned, Mary had already died. Mr. Miller had discovered that Mary had married one of his friends, David Jones, that they had had Nila, and Mary had been very happy in her marriage. Mr. Miller was both sad and joyful—grieved that he never got to see Mary again but pleased that she had had a good life.

Mr. Miller often told Nila that she was the spitting image of her mother. So Nila was the golden child of Legacy High in Mr. Miller's eyes. Everyone knew this, including Mrs. Carver and Dawn Gale Williams.

The mere mention of Mr. Miller's name made Dawn stop, turn, and stomp to Mrs. Carver's desk. Dawn threw her things on the table and plunked herself down in the chair, sulking beside Mrs. Carver's desk.

Nila breathed a sigh of relief. It must have been noticeable because Blake asked, "Issues with you two?"

"Not really. She is the princess of Legacy, she hates me, and makes my life miserable as often as she possibly can," Nila said with a sarcastic smile.

"Well then, you need to let me know the next time she harasses you. I got your back," Blake said trying to make the comment sound like a joke. But Nila thought he might just be serious.

Nila smiled, "I'll hold you to that."

"Okay then," Blake replied.

Nila and Blake began to work on their sketches for Mrs. Carver. Knowing that she had already been chosen, Nila did her sketch anyway. She sketched an unsuspecting Blake. They talked and laughed as they worked. Nila finished and closed her sketchpad.

"Let me see," Blake insisted.

"No, it's really not that good," a panicky Nila replied. She hoped that he would drop it. She really didn't want to reveal the sketch to Blake.

"I'm not giving up. Let me see. Please," Blake begged.

Nila reluctantly and slowly showed the picture to him.

"Wow! This is awesome. How'd you do this? I didn't pose. In fact, I was constantly moving. It looks just like me. If Mrs. Carver doesn't keep it, can I have it?"

Nila was both flustered and flattered. She couldn't believe her ears. "Sure. But you don't have to take it to be nice."

"I'm not, really. I love it."

Mrs. Carver called time. She went around the class picking up everyone's sketches except Nila's. So when Mrs. Carver bypassed Nila's sketch, Nila handed it over to Blake. Blake smiled and thanked her. He carefully stowed it in his sketchpad.

Dawn had watched the two throughout art class. Mrs. Carver intentionally picked up Dawn's sketch last. As she picked up the sketch, she leaned in and whispered to

Dawn, "You best leave them be. Don't be messing with Nila. You hear me?"

Dawn just glared at Mrs. Carver, grabbed her things, and shoved her chair back, letting it tip over on the floor. Mrs. Carver's patience was growing thin. "Miss Williams, watch your step." Dawn turned and walked away with her nose in the air. Luckily, Mrs. Carver's distractions helped Nila and Blake get out of class way before Dawn.

Blake walked Nila to her next class, which was literature, one of her favorites and right next to Blake's history class, which was great for Blake. Apparently, he was a big history buff. Nila entered her class and Blake went into his. Nila turned back to get one last glimpse of him. Her heart fell.

Holy crap! Nila thought as she saw Dawn walk into Blake's history class. Nila could hardly keep her mind on her lit class; she was too busy trying to keep her thoughts from wandering into the classroom next door. *What was going on? Where was Blake sitting? Was Dawn putting the moves on him? If so, was he enjoying it?* Nila caught a word here and there, enough to know that they were discussing Edgar Allan Poe, one of her favorite authors. So, it was very unlike her to be distracted while there was a discussion of Poe going on in her vicinity.

Finally, the bell rang. None too soon. Nila was starving, and lunch was next. She was also dying to see Blake again. Sherry was waiting just outside Nila's class. Mr. Evans, Nila's lit teacher who had been her lit teacher the past two years, stopped her on the way out. "Nila, is everything alright?"

"Yeah, sure. Why do you ask?"

"Well, you seemed to be very distracted today. It's very unlike you not to pay full attention in class."

"I'm fine, really. Just really hungry. I missed breakfast this morning."

"Okay, then. If you're sure. Enjoy lunch," Mr. Evans said with an unconvinced look about him.

"Thanks, Mr. Evans," Nila said as she rushed out the door to meet Sherry.

"Damn, girl. You just missed your dream guy," Sherry said.

"Really, which way did he go?"

"He went back upstairs."

"Oh," Nila disappointedly replied as she and Sherry began to walk toward the lunchroom.

"Oh, now. It's okay. I'm sure you'll see him again some time today."

"Yeah, I guess you're right," Nila replied with a smile. "I did have art with him this morning."

"No way!"

"Yeah."

"Did you get to talk to him at all?"

"Actually, he sat at my table with me."

"That crappy little table you sit at every year?"

"The one and the same."

"Did you guys talk a lot?"

"Yeah, actually we did. Nothing significant though, just small-talk. I did a sketch of him in class. He wanted it. I gave it to him."

"No way!"

"Yeah. I think he really liked it," Nila said with a smile. It was a smile that Sherry didn't think that she'd ever seen on Nila's face before.

"Well, come on in. I'm starving," Sherry said as she pulled open the cafeteria door.

The two girls dropped their things off at their usual table and got in line. "Great! Pizza day!" Sherry exclaimed like a 3-year-old. Nila always admired the way that small things excited Sherry.

"I'm glad it's something good since I missed my breakfast because someone kept honking their horn," Nila said, while rolling her eyes like a drama queen, which she did when she was being sarcastic with Sherry.

"What! You're the one who overslept and almost made us late," Sherry said as she playfully leaned into Nila. The two girls laughed and got their trays. As usual, the eyes of all the guys in the lunchroom were on Sherry as she pulled her lunch money from her bra and paid for lunch with it. They turned to walk back to their table when Nila almost dropped her tray. She couldn't believe what she was seeing.

Chapter 3

"That damn Dawn sure works fast, doesn't she," Sherry said disgustedly. Nila's eyes were fixed on Blake standing with some guys she knew and Dawn Williams hanging all over him. Nila suddenly lost her appetite. She walked directly to the trashcan beside Dawn and Blake and threw her tray in it—food and all. Blake was surprised. He hadn't even noticed that she was in the cafeteria until he saw her walk out of the line with her tray in hand. Nila turned and walked away.

"Nila, wait!" Blake desperately called out to her. But Nila stormed out, not even stopping to get her things.

Sherry put her tray down and walked over to Dawn. Blake started to say something, but Sherry wasn't at all interested. She ignored Blake and grabbed Dawn by the hair. Before anyone could react, Sherry threw Dawn to the floor and sat atop her punching the hell out of her. Blake and a few of the guys he was with pulled Sherry off Dawn before any teachers saw what was happening. Sherry resisted for a minute or two, then adjusted her clothes, and rubbed her hands across her hair. She went to pick up her tray and turned to see Dawn missing hair, crying like a baby, and bleeding profusely. Sherry said through gritted teeth, "Don't screw with Nila. I got your number, bitch."

Dawn turned and ran to the first teacher she saw, Mr. Addams. Dawn gave him the entire spiel of what Sherry had done and said. Dawn was always crying wolf, so Mr. Addams didn't know what to think when he looked over and saw Sherry quietly sitting at her table calmly talking to her friends and eating her lunch with not so much as one hair out of place. Mr. Addams had come to blows with Dawn and her father over Dawn's failing history grades the year before. So, it's understandable why he wasn't a big fan of Dawn's anyway. Dawn had told so many lies about so many girls that she didn't like that the teachers could no longer take her word for anything.

"Well, Dawn, do you have any witnesses, because it really doesn't look like Sherry's been scrapping lately?" Mr. Addams asked suspiciously.

"Of course, I do! The guys who pulled that crazy bitch off me," Dawn snapped back.

"Shall we go speak to them first?"

"Sure," Dawn replied sarcastically.

Dawn pranced over to Blake and the others who were still standing in line with him. "Blake would you please tell Mr. Addams what that crazy Sherry Parker did to me?"

"What do you mean? What happened to you anyway? You look like crap? Hey, is that fake blood?" Blake replied.

Dawn was mortified. No guy had ever said that she looked like crap before. She wondered if he didn't know who he was talking to. What was his deal anyway?

"Well," Mr. Addams interjected. "Miss Williams said that Miss Parker just attacked her and you boys pulled Miss Parker off her."

"When?" Blake asked with a convincingly puzzled look.

"Just now, you fool. What are you trying to pull anyway? And the rest of you, you know exactly what I'm talking about. What's wrong with all of you? You're all a bunch of losers!" Dawn yelled.

"Then why would you be hanging out here with us anyway?" one of the boys asked.

"I was hanging out with Blake, not you idiots," Dawn snapped.

"And yet you expect these boys to vouch for you, Miss Williams? I really don't know what you're trying to pull, but I suggest you clean yourself up and have a seat with your usual crowd," Mr. Addams prompted.

This scenario would have been karma at its best, Nila thought, as her fantasy came to an end and she found herself in the girl's restroom nearest the cafeteria. Actually, after Nila had tossed her lunch in the trash and headed toward the door, Blake had called out to her, and Sherry did walk over to Dawn and whisper in her ear, "Leave Nila alone. Don't go screwing around with her. I got your number, bitch."

Nila knew that Sherry would do something. Sherry was very protective of Nila. She had been since Kindergarten when Troy Austin pushed Nila down in the dirt and took her ice cream. Sherry ran over and pummeled him. He never spoke to Nila or Sherry since then. Of course, Sherry got into some deep crap for that. But she has always had Nila's back no matter what. This was no exception.

Dawn retaliated by pushing Sherry. Sherry just laughed at her and asked, "Why aren't you with your usual bunch of wieners? Are you slumming it today? This isn't your type of crowd. These are my buds."

Dawn replied snidely, "Yeah, and you've probably had them all. Right?"

Sherry just continued to laugh and asked, "Wouldn't you love to be me?"

With her nose in the air, Dawn turned and mumbled, "Losers," to Sherry and her buds.

Sherry warned Dawn once again to stay away, not to mess with Nila, and to stay with her own crowd.

Blake tried to explain to Sherry what had really happened, but Sherry wouldn't hear any of it. She waved him off with her hand and shook her head from side to side. She dropped her tray off at her table and left the cafeteria, hunting for Nila. Sherry had a pretty good idea that Nila was in the closest restroom. Sherry knew Nila like the back of her hand. She knew that Nila was very private and wouldn't want anyone seeing her so upset and ask questions.

Sherry pushed open the door to the bathroom closest to the cafeteria and called out to Nila, "Come on, girl. I know you're in here." Sherry checked underneath the stalls until she found a pair of feet in a cute pair of tan sandals that looked familiar—Nila's feet, Nila's sandals. "Nila, I can see your feet." Sherry continued to plead with Nila, "You know, coaxing stray cats from under houses is easier than trying to coax you out from that damn stall. Come on, Nila."

Nila didn't say anything. Instead, she slowly opened the stall door with her head hung about as low as Sherry had ever seen a head hung before. Nila just fell into Sherry's arms and wept profoundly.

"Why did I dream about him in such a way? And then he came here. Why did he talk to me and act interested and then let that bitch hang all over him? Is this some kind of cruel karmic fate? What did I do in a past life that was so bad? I have the worst luck."

"Girl, that you do. But if you want the truth, I don't think that Blake was letting Dawn hang all over him. I think it was more like trying to get gum off your shoes. When I went over, he wriggled uncomfortably by her. You know, kind of like someone trying to shake off a spider or something. I think it caught him off guard and he just didn't want to blatantly be mean to her. Don't worry, though, I smacked that spider right off him and back to her own kind."

"You hit her?" Nila asked through the tears, as flashes of her fantasy rushed through her head.

"Not physically. It's too early in the year to get suspended. I slapped her around with words and warnings."

"What did Blake have to say?"

"He tried to talk to me, but I waved him on like a stinky fart and came out to find you. I do think that he's really worried, if that helps any."

"Yeah, I guess it does a little. But I'm still seriously pissed."

"I tell you what. Let's go back and get our crap. I'll text Kevin and see if he's into ditching today. If he is, we'll find him and take off. If he's not, we'll just bolt ourselves. Since neither one of us are getting lunch, we'll stop at The Burger Joint or Big Bud's Burgers and grab a burger. Then we'll spend the afternoon at the lake. You wanted to ditch anyway, right?"

"You know, that actually sounds great," Nila replied as she wiped away the last few tears.

Sherry helped Nila regain composure and get presentable. The two meandered back to the cafeteria arms, around each other, back to their table. Sherry tossed her lunch, thinking what a shame. *This damn school hardly ever has anything good to eat, and today of all days and I have to toss my lunch.* Sherry methodically threw her food in the trash can, took her tray and silverware to the dishwasher and gave the dishwasher a half smile, half grimace thinking about the pizza that now lay in the trash. Turning to Dawn's table, Sherry gave Dawn a triumphant look as if to say, you know what's good for you, don't ya?

Nila was struggling to keep her composure while trying to gather her things and not look in Blake's direction. Even though she didn't look at Blake, she knew he was looking at her. She could feel the weight of his stare. She could feel in her stomach that he would be coming over soon if she didn't get out of there. Blake's eyes pierced her flesh, making her feel tingles of electricity all over her body. Nila could feel desperation in Blake's eyes that gave her an eerie sensation even though she couldn't see him looking at her. The feeling reminded her of something, but she couldn't quite put her finger on it.

Suddenly, Nila had flashes of the wooded area from her dreams—dense forest, heavy fog, and barking dogs. She felt desperate and fearful, knowing she had to get away. Then she heard a faint voice whisper in her ear, "Lorelei is coming. Run fast, girl. Run fast!"

Nila bolted with what she had in her hands—her purse and her sketchpad—leaving her lit, math, and biology books behind. Sherry turned toward Nila just as Nila flew out the door like a frightened bird. Sherry glanced at Blake and was surprised to see that he looked disheartened and alone. She wanted to cry for him. She had never felt an emotion so strong before in her life. She picked up Nila's books that she had left behind and chased Nila to her little, beat-up, black car.

When Sherry caught up to Nila, Nila was sitting by the car's back passenger-side tire. Knees drawn up into her chest, heart beating wildly, and fear in her eyes—Sherry had never seen Nila like this. It reminded her of one of those advertisements of abused animals. That was it! Nila looked and acted like an abused and fearful dog.

"What is it with you today?"

"I don't know. I just felt frightened and trapped. I could feel Blake staring at me. Then I started having hallucinations or something. It was like flashbacks or something about that thicket from those crazy dreams. I felt the same sensations as I did when I was dreaming. I could hear the dogs barking, I saw the fog and the woods. There was no cafeteria and no kids. It was just me and the feeling of being watched and chased. Then I heard a whisper in the wind."

"A whisper? Girl, what are you talking about? Who whispered? You been smokin' something?"

"Of course not! I don't know who whispered. Nobody, I think. It was more like the wind whistling that sounded like words. It sounded like 'Lorelei is coming, run fast.'"

"What the hell does that mean? Who is Lorelei?"

"I don't know. Just find Kevin, and let's get out of here quick. Please," Nila begged.

"Okay, okay. Don't get your panties in a twist. Get in, and I'll text him."

Sherry texted Kevin as Nila fell into the back seat of Sherry's car. "Where u at. U wanna go 2 the lake." The girls sat in silence as they waited for a reply for what seemed like an eternity. It was only two minutes.

Kevin texted, "Sure. Where r u."

"Parkin lot."

"B there n 5."

"K." Sherry finished the text, looked up, and updated Nila. "Okay, he's on his way, and then we'll hit a burger joint."

"Sounds good to me. Thanks."

Nila sat in the back seat, waiting in silence. She got in the back out of respect. After all, it was Sherry's boyfriend. He did have longer legs than she did, and she really wanted to be in the background for a while. Kevin came barreling out of Legacy High School's doors like he owned the place. He was so cocky. Nila figured he had to have that type of attitude to keep up and to put up with Sheryl Agnes Parker.

Sherry hated her name. She never gave Nila a reason why she hated her first name—just that she did. But, Agnes. Well, Sherry told Nila she associated the name Agnes with the movie about a nun. Sounded like an old woman's name, she said. While actually it was—she was named for her grandmother. Nila told Sherry that she should be proud to be named for such a woman.

In southern culture, it's common to name children for other family members. Nila was named after some ancestor who lived in Legacy in the 1700s—Nila Anne Jones—her full name. The woman was on her father's side. It was a bit disturbing to Nila because this woman had died young. She never even married. Nila reminded Sherry of that when Sherry complained about her name.

Kevin hopped into the car and gave Sherry a sensual and lengthy kiss. Nila cleared her throat, "Guys. PDA." They pulled back almost embarrassed but not quite.

"Sorry, Niles," Kevin apologized as he snickered like a 5-year-old caught with his hands down his pants. "So, let's go to the lake."

Kevin noticed immediately that Nila was upset but never let on. He was considerate that way. He never pried but would always listen if someone needed an ear. Nila appreciated that, especially now.

"Hold on there, cowboy," Sherry interjected. "We didn't get lunch. We're stopping off for a burger first. Where to Nila?"

"Don't care," Nila replied softly.

"The Burger Joint? It's closer."

"Sure, that's fine."

"Okay, The Burger Joint it is. You want anything, Kev?"

"Sure. Burger sounds good."

Kevin never turned down food. He had lunch before Nila and Sherry. They both knew he couldn't possibly be hungry, and yet he still wanted a burger.

Nila looked at Kevin in the car that day with new light for some reason. He seemed like someone she could depend on. She had never thought of him being dependable. He was a good listener, but didn't seem dependable until then. She thought that if she needed him, he would be there for her. Why did she now see him so differently, she thought to herself. He didn't look any different. He looked the same as always. He wore a cowboy hat with a sweat ring around the base from many long hours on the farm. He wore the same scuffed-up cowboy boots. Same type t-shirt he typically wore. Same torn, faded blue jeans. Same shoulder-length, soft, brown, wavy hair. Same deep-brown eyes. Same rough hands from hard farming. And same sensual bass voice. Nila had to admit— she was a little jealous of Sherry. Nila had always thought that Kevin was good looking. She was quite surprised when he and Sherry had hooked up. They were so totally different. He was a cowboy, a farm boy, very country. She was very trampy, very punk, everything not country. But somehow they worked.

The next thing Nila knew they were in the drive-thru at The Burger Joint, and Sherry was saying, "Nila. Hey girl. Back to Earth. What do you want?"

"I'm sorry, I'm not sure. Order yours first."

"Um, we already have."

"Oh. Well, just a burger, fries, and a diet whatever, then."

Sherry repeated Nila's order to the cashier. The cashier gave Sherry the total. Sherry paid, collected the food, and headed toward the lake.

The lake was a local hangout for the kids of Legacy High. It was close to school and very beautiful. There were trees of all kinds at the lake; the most beautiful of all were the Laurel bushes when in full bloom.

Nila was so lost in thought that she had forgotten how hungry she was until she smelled those burgers and fries. Her mouth watered, and she couldn't wait to take a bite of that big, juicy burger.

The three finally reached the lake. Sherry and Kevin excitedly jumped out of the car. Nila poured of it. Kevin grabbed the food, and Sherry retrieved a homemade, patchwork quilt from the back seat. She was always prepared for anything that required the use of a quilt. Sherry spread the old quilt out on a level spot just at the edge of the lake under the shade of a willow tree.

They sat down on the quilt. Kevin quickly distributed the food. Nila couldn't remember being this hungry since her mother died—when she was so distraught that she couldn't eat for a week and a half. Her grandmother was worried that Nila was going to wither up and blow away.

Nila rapidly unwrapped her burger and ate it so quickly she barely tasted it. She had eaten her entire burger and fries before Kevin even finished one of his burgers and Sherry was still working on hers. No one said a word until they finished their food. Finally, Nila confessed, "I was so hungry, I didn't even chew. Thanks, Sherry. That really hit the spot."

"Oh, you're welcome girl. Any time. I'm just glad to see you back in the land of the living. You were so upset. I've never seen you like this over a guy before."

"A guy? What did I miss this morning?" Kevin asked.

"You'll have to ask Nila," Sherry said. She had never betrayed Nila's trust, and she wasn't about to start that day.

Kevin looked from Sherry to Nila not wanting to ask Nila. But curiosity got the best of him. Nila thought only for a moment before deciding she should tell Kevin. She felt like she could trust him and maybe even get some good guy advice from him about the whole Blake situation. So Nila spilled her guts. She told Kevin everything. Nila explained to him about the dreams and what had happened in the cafeteria. Sherry was astonished. She couldn't believe that her bff, Nila, decided to trust Kevin enough to confide him.

Kevin didn't act surprised at all. He just looked at her and said, "Niles, its fate. My granny always talks about second chances in another life, karma, and the chance to set things straight. She says that we get to come back and try to get things right. We all have soul mates, and each time we come back to be born again in a new body, we would always find that person. She says that sometimes a man may come back as a woman, and sometimes a woman may come back as a man. But that don't matter because the soul don't care, it's neither male nor female. I think he and you are soul mates. You should really talk to Granny about this. She could probably help."

Nila and Sherry were shocked at Kevin's thoughtful response. They couldn't believe what they were hearing. "Thanks," Nila finally said, "maybe I will give her a call."

Somehow, what Kevin had said made her feel much better. Not quite like herself, but almost. As Nila's mood began to lighten, the three laughed and joked. Sherry and Kevin tried to keep the PDA down because Nila was there. Nila thought to herself, *They must be soul mates. They seem so perfect for one another even though they are so different.* Nila didn't say anything about the PDA; she just smiled and was happy for her friends. That day, she decided to take him out of the acquaintance category and put Kevin in her friends category.

Kevin jumped up and suggested, "Let's go swimming, girls."

"Okay," the two best friends said as they stripped down to their panties and bras.

A short distance away, Nila was being watched.

Chapter 4

Blake had been so upset by Nila's obvious distress to Dawn hanging on him that he signed himself out of school in hopes of finding her. On his way out, he caught a guy he had made friends with that day who was also friends of Nila and Sherry. He was a tall, lanky boy with an average build; short, messy, brown hair; and soft, brown eyes. He wore torn jeans and a black band t-shirt with motorcycle boots. What was really strange about this boy was his British accent. Obviously, he hadn't lived in Legacy very long.

"Hey, Dude, can you tell me where Nila Jones lives?" Blake asked.

"Sure," the boy replied as he proceeded to give him directions to her home.

Armed with this information, Blake decided to go to Nila's house to make sure that she was okay. He wasn't sure what the reception would be like but he was willing to take the chance. All the way to Nila Jones' house, he wondered what he would say. *How would she react? Would she let him explain? Let him make things right?* He had to try no matter what her reaction was. Finally, he reached Nila's house and slowly drove up the driveway, almost reluctantly. He parked and got out of his car. He walked to the door, playing in his mind the perfect scenario—Nila letting him in, letting him explain, and understanding.

He paused briefly, taking a long breath before knocking on the old, wooden door of the farmhouse. From within the house he heard the elderly voice of a woman call out, "Come on in, it's open."

He turned the knob and walked slowly through the doorway saying, "Hello?"

An elderly woman came from the kitchen, wiping her hands on her apron, "Yes, can I help you?"

"Yes ma'am, I'm looking for Nila Jones."

"Well, dear boy, she's supposed to be at school," the old lady replied puzzled.

"Um, well, I don't want to get her into any trouble but her and her friend, Sherry, left at lunch," Blake told her.

"My guess is that if they've skipped school, then they're most likely at the lake," she replied in a nonchalant manner. "I'm Nila's grandmother, Ruth Jones," the old lady said as she reached out her hand to Blake.

He reached forward, and politely took her hand up to his mouth, brushed it with a light kiss and slightly bowed. It was a bit traditional, but it was what was instilled in him since childhood. "Pleased to meet you, ma'am. My name is Blake Billings. I'm new to the area. I only just met Nila today at Legacy High, but I was quite taken with her. I think that she may have left school upset. It had something to do with a Dawn someone. I just wanted to make sure that she was okay."

"What a nice boy you are. Are you from the south? You greet a lady like a true southern gentleman. How sweet of you to check on her. I'm sure she's fine though. Nila has been through a lot. She's a strong girl."

"Thank you. I'm from Massachusetts, but my family roots are from here in Legacy. My family carried on the southern traditions to their children and grandchildren and so on."

"Well, Mr. Blake, would you like a glass of sweet iced tea?" Ruth asked gesturing toward the kitchen.

"No, ma'am. Thank you. I really want to check on Nila. Can you tell me how to get to the lake?" Blake politely asked.

"Well, of course. I'm old, not senile," the old lady said jokingly. Then she gave Blake the directions using more hand gestures than actual words.

"Thank you very much, Mrs. Jones," Blake said as he bowed his head slightly to her.

"Oh, you're very welcome. You're welcome in my house any time. It was so nice to meet you. Now you come back and see an old lady again, you hear," she said as she smiled and flushed like a schoolgirl. It had been many years since a young man had made her feel giddy.

"Thanks again," Blake said as he walked out the front door of the old farmhouse where Nila Jones lived. He dismounted the old, creaky, front porch and walked to his car. He jumped in and drove to the lake. All the way to the lake he thought only of Nila—her beauty, her voice, and how familiar she was. He finally reached the lake but had no idea where to look or even what kind of car they were in. He decided to let his heart guide him. He by passed an old, beat-up, black car not realizing that it was Sherry's car. However, he felt that he should go back. He parked his car and walked back toward the black car. He was unsure of how to approach Nila and, for that matter, unsure of her reception of him.

As he neared the little, black car, he heard the laughter of the two girls. He quietly moved toward Nila's laughter. He found himself behind a tree, watching Nila like a common peeping Tom. He could not avert his eyes from her as she undressed. Excitement grew within him—a feeling he had not felt in so long. Nila first unbuttoned her white, cotton blouse, revealing the outer edges of her small, rounded breasts that were peeking out of her bra. A small, golden, Celtic knot hung carefree between them, sparkling in the sun like a tiny star. Then she wriggled her skirt down her beautiful, slender legs that were tanned from a long, hot summer of gardening, until the skirt was on the ground at her feet. She and Sherry wasted no time running to the lake's edge as Kevin was already waiting for them in the crystal, clear water. It didn't take Kevin any time to lose his clothes.

This was not unusual for the girls. When they went to the lake alone, they discarded all of their clothing, opting for total skinny-dipping. They weren't prudish about their bodies. Blake admired Nila for her boldness. He looked on as the three splashed around in the water. He couldn't look away from Nila's beauty for one second. Her body was almost completely submerged in the water. Only her head, shoulders, and the top of her breasts glistened in the warm sunshine. Water beads ran down her like streams of raindrops on a windowpane during a thunderstorm. And like the electricity in the air of a thunderstorm, Blake felt it run through him. He had waited so long for her. Nila's wet, black hair flowed down the back of her neck and shoulders with a few stray strands tickling her face. He was so wrapped up in the beauty of Nila that he slipped and broke a twig with his foot as he caught his balance.

Kevin called out, "Hey! Who's the peeping Tom? Hope you're getting your eyes full."

Embarrassed, Blake turned and tried to sneak away unseen but Nila knew him even from a distance. "Wait," she called out to him. As if she had a physical hold over him, he had to obey her command and stop. He slowly turned as she called out, "Blake, is that you?"

"Yes, your grandmother told me that you might be here."

"My grandmother isn't home. She went to visit my aunt. She won't be back until tonight," Nila replied suspiciously.

"Ruth Jones, right? Small but stern, gray hair in a bun, eyes just like yours?" Blake called back to Nila.

"Well, yes. But why would she tell you where I would be?" Nila questioned.

"I sweet-talked her."

Sherry nudged Nila, "Go talk to him, girl. What are you waitin' on? Obviously he's concerned and cares or he wouldn't be here."

"Yeah, take a chance Niles. Soul mates, remember? Don't be too hard on him. Let him explain. We'll swim to the far end of the lake for a while. You know, PDA and all," Kevin said while smiling.

Sherry gave Nila a shrug and a pleading look. "Okay. Thanks, guys," Nila replied in an uncertain tone.

"Sure thing," Sherry said, as she and Kevin turned to swim away.

Nila slowly waded out of the lake moving toward Blake.

He thought she looked like a goddess, emerging gracefully from the water. He wanted to fall at her feet and worship her forever. She walked toward him, and he made his way from behind the tree to approach her. Nila asked, "What are you doing stalking me anyway? I thought you'd be hanging with Dawn," Nila sniped.

"Can I please explain?" Blake begged.

"You can try."

Blake could barely keep his thoughts straight as he stared at her still-dripping body from the lake water. "I don't know Dawn except from class today. She came up to me and asked why I was so taken with you. I told her that you had a great personality, was beautiful, and I felt that we had an instant connection. She then said that you may be pretty but you were a total prude and she could show me a good time. I told her that I wasn't interested. All the while I was trying to get away from her. She was like nasty fly tape. The more I moved to get away the harder she stuck. I told her that I didn't have any desire in her showing me her rendition of a good time. I just wanted to be with you."

Nila couldn't help herself. She believed every word Blake said. She totally believed him without question, but she didn't want him to know that he had won so easily. "How do I know you're not feeding me a line? Besides, what makes you think that I'm that interested in you?"

"For starters, you throw your lunch away as soon as you get it while giving us a go-to-hell look. I assumed that was because you liked me and was maybe a bit jealous," he said while walking toward Nila, backing her up against a tree.

"I may have just been pissed at Dawn. It may have had nothing to do with you. And really, I'm not interested in you," Nila said trying to play it cool while she felt the tree bark scratching against her back. She didn't want to seem eager for his affection, even though she wanted to be wrapped in his arms for an eternity.

Blake placed his hands on the tree on either side of Nila's head with her body pressed between the tree and his rock-hard body. She could tell that he was excited, and this pleased her. She wondered if he could tell that she was just as excited by him. He leaned in close and whispered into her right ear, his face almost touching hers, so close that the soft waves of his hair tickled the side of her cheek. He said, "Oh, I think you're interested."

Nila tried to get away by trying to move under his left arm. But Blake reached out and grabbed both of Nila's wrists holding them above her head making resistance impossible. Nila was terribly excited at his forcefulness. He leaned in close and whispered, "Why do you tremble beneath my touch? Why do your lips pout like they want to be kissed by me? Why do you look at me with longing in your eyes? Why do you breathe so heavy?"

Nila knew that everything Blake said was true. She was trembling, did want him to kiss her, and was breathing heavy with anticipation of what might come next. She couldn't argue with him. He had totally taken control, and she had lost total control. Nila was pressed against the tree, Blake pinning her to the tree. She couldn't move. She wanted him so badly.

Blake leaned in close once again. Nila thought for sure that he was going to kiss her; instead, he stepped back and let go of her. But before he could take even two steps back, Nila acted on pure instinct and couldn't believe her own actions. She reached out and grabbed Blake by the hand, pulling him back into her, once again being pinned between the tree and Blake's hardness. She kissed him with a passion and hunger that couldn't be satisfied. The feelings that she had during her dreams came flooding into her body with force and power. She let herself be swept away by the euphoria. Blake returned her kiss with the same passion and hunger. He took her face into his hands and held her firmly so that there was no escape until he was ready to release her. Blake kissed her so deeply that Nila just knew that she would die from the pure pleasure of it.

Blake finally pulled his lips from hers, "I thought you weren't interested?"

"I guess I lied a little," Nila smiled. Blake smiled and released her face. He dropped his left hand and took her right hand in his. He then led her trembling, wet, half-naked, excited body to the patchwork quilt spread on the ground at the lake's edge. They sat, Nila unsure of what was to come next. But it didn't matter. She would go wherever Blake led her. Nila saw everything around her in a new light. She saw the world like she had never seen it before. It was as if she had been in a foggy dream her entire life to awaken to a clear, bright, sunny day. Everything around her appeared so clear, clean, and crisp. All five senses seemed alive, especially her sense of touch. Blake's hands brought her body to life, a liveliness that she had never experienced.

Noticing that Nila was trembling, Blake took his t-shirt off and gave it to her to wear. "Here, you're shivering."

Nila was cold but more excited. Nila didn't want him to quit kissing her, touching her, and making her feel this extreme emotion. She wanted more. Nila thought to herself, *Damn, if I put on his shirt does that mean he's finished? Is my body not pleasing to him? Or is he just being that nobleman that I know he is?* Nila reluctantly took his shirt and slipped it over her head.

Nila was amazed at how beautifully his body was built. He was lightly tan and muscular, not bulky, but firm and lean with definition. Nila studied his body. *My God, he is an Adonis. He is the most beautiful thing I've ever seen.*

Then she took notice of the wonderful scent on his shirt. At that moment, she understood exactly what pheromones were and the effect they had on people. She thought he had the most wonderful musky scent. It was like nothing she had ever smelled before.

Blake admired Nila with a smile, wondering what she was thinking. She took so long to respond to him because her brain was trying to process all of these new emotions. Finally, Nila realized it had been a long minute and she still hadn't responded to Blake. "Thank you," she smiled.

He was so taken by her smile. It was innocent, yet seductive. He had long understood the emotions and sensations that came with such intimacy. However, he was unprepared for the effect that she had on him. He wanted to maintain control until Nila had gotten to know and understand him, until he was sure that she was truly ready for what he had to offer her. But he was having great difficulty when he touched her, smelled her, and looked at her. He was so unprepared at seeing her in her underwear—wet and beautiful. He could barely control what was so natural for a man.

"I'm sorry," Blake said. "I didn't mean to go so fast. I just needed you to know what really happened this morning. I really needed to know if you felt the same way about me as I do for you. Again, I apologize."

Those words caused all of Nila's insecurities to disappear like a nightmare in the light of a new day. "Why are you apologizing? I'm the one who kissed you. I really don't do that. I'm not easy. I just. Well, it just feels like I've known you forever. It felt so natural. I apologize."

Blake reached up and lightly caressed Nila's face with the back o his hand. Nila's eyes automatically shut and she was swept away in her emotions. She leaned into his hand with her face and drew in a deep breath, taking in the wonderful scent of his skin. Blake smiled, knowing the effect he had over her. She slowly opened her eyes as Blake dropped his hand onto her thigh. His warm hand on her thigh made electricity flow through her body like lightning strikes. Blake slowly drew his hand back, dragging it across the length of her leg. Nila longed for him to put his hands all over her body, but she didn't want him to think badly of her.

"Nila Jones, you are something else. I think I like you," he smiled.

"You think?" Nila giggled. "I think I like you, too."

"Yeah, I got that when you kissed me." After a slight pause, Blake continued, "So do you swim in your underwear often?"

"Only if there's guys around. If it's just Sherry and I, we skinny-dip."

"Well then, too bad Sherry's boyfriend was here," Blake said as he laughed and leaned into her shoulder playfully nudging her.

Nila smiled, "Yeah."

Blake asked, "Where did Sherry and her boyfriend go?"

"Sherry and Kevin wanted to give us some privacy."

"So you and Sherry close, huh?"

"Yeah, since Kindergarten. She's always watched out for me, always been there. She's more like a sister than a friend. Kevin's a good guy, too. They've only been dating a couple of months. I think he may be the one. She goes through guys like hotcakes. I love her, but she's kind of the school slut. It's well known and she won't deny it."

"Your grandmother don't mind you hanging with her?" Blake asked.

"No. She and my dad trust me to do what I know is right in my heart. They know I don't give into peer pressure. I am my own person, good or bad," Nila replied.

"Your grandmother and dad know you go skinny-dipping?" Blake questioned.

"Yeah, my family isn't as prudish and backward as some in the area. They're open-minded but still traditional southern in some ways. I don't want to pry, and you can tell me it's none of my business if you want, but what exactly happened to your parents?"

"They were trapped in a house fire. That's it plain and simple. They were great parents, very kind and compassionate, understanding and loving. I really miss them."

"I'm really very sorry. If you ever want or need to talk about it, I'll be there for you. But I won't mention it again. I don't like to bring up painful and hurtful subjects to people. I would like to hear more about them when and if you want to tell me. They sound great."

"Thank you. I may just take you up on that. It is painful and I don't want to get into that mindset today. I just want to spend some time with you and enjoy myself."

"Okay, sounds good. Do you want to swim. Take a walk or something?"

"Sure. Let's swim," Blake suggested.

Nila pulled Blake's shirt up over her head. Blake took off his shoes, socks, and pants. They raced hand-in-hand to the water's edge. They played, laughed, swam, and splashed for the longest time. They had so much fun, totally lost in the warm, sunny afternoon.

Sherry and Kevin returned, and the four swam together until dusk. They waded out of the lake and back to the old quilt where they took turns drying off with it. The girls went behind a nearby tree and shucked their wet underwear and slipped on their dry clothes. However, the guys weren't as modest as the two girls, they stayed there at the quilt and changed.

Nila caught a glimpse of Blake's nakedness. She had never seen a man's body before—at least not in person, just in movies. He was magnificent, god-like. Nila felt slightly guilty for looking at Blake instead of averting her eyes. The guilt was replaced by embarrassment when Sherry caught her.

"Nila, you better not be looking at Kevin," Sherry joked, knowing good and well who Nila was looking at.

"Shush. Don't be so loud, they'll hear you. Trust me. Kevin is not where my eyes were aimed."

The girls laughed and finished dressing. "So how'd it go?" Sherry asked.

"It was great," Nila briefly told Sherry what had transpired between the two young lovers.

Sherry elbowed Nila and said, "I told ya he wasn't interested in Dawn."

They ran back and met the boys at the quilt. "So, I guess I'll see you tomorrow," Nila shyly said to Blake.

"Do you need a ride? Sherry already has to take Kevin back home, right? I could run you back to your place, if you'd like," Blake suggested.

Nila looked at Sherry. Sherry smiled and shook her head in agreement. "Yeah, that would be nice if it won't put you out," Nila answered.

"Not at all. It would be an honor to be seen riding around with such a beautiful girl," Blake told Nila. "My car is back this way," Blake said as he gestured toward the area where he had left his car. The two couples said goodbye to each other. Sherry and Kevin got into her car, and Nila and Blake walked in the direction of his car. As Nila and Blake walked, Blake's right hand dropped down and wrapped it around Nila's hand. She loved the feeling of being touched by him. She glanced over and smiled at him, and he smiled back.

They reached Blake's car. He pointed and said, "There it is."

Nila was astounded. It was a beautiful, old car. "Wow!" she exclaimed

"It has been in my family for years. It was purchased new in the 1930's by a great, great something," he explained.

"It's absolutely beautiful."

"Thank you," Blake said as he opened the door for Nila.

She got in, and he shut the door behind her. He walked around to the driver's side and got in. He began to drive. Before she knew it, they were at the old farmhouse that she knew so well. Blake pulled into the driveway, parked, and switched off the lights and ignition. He turned to her and said, "Nila, thank you for letting me explain about today. Thank you for the stolen kisses. And thank you for the wonderful evening."

"No, thank you. I had a great time. I enjoyed the kisses, the swimming, everything. I'm sorry I acted like such a brat earlier today. Dawn just gets the best of me. When I saw you with her, I thought I had lost you before I ever had the chance to have you."

"That's okay. It's actually kind of flattering. I know that it's crazy to say and it feels like things are moving really fast, but I feel like I've known you since the dawn of time. And you're not going to lose me," Blake said as he leaned in for one more stolen kiss. This time, it was gentle and sweet, not so heated and aggressive like the kisses earlier. That was okay. Nila liked this, too.

When he pulled back, Nila whispered breathlessly, "I should go in now."

"I'll see you tomorrow. Maybe you can do another sketch of me in art."

"Oh, crap!" Nila exclaimed. "I forgot Mrs. Carver. I was supposed to help her this afternoon."

"I'm sure she will be fine about it. I get the feeling you are kind of her pet."

Nila smiled knowing that his statement was true. She didn't know how to respond so she said, "Thanks again, Blake Billings."

"No prob."

With that, Nila opened the door to the beautiful, old car; took a few steps toward her front porch; and she turned to get one last look at her young nobleman. He waved at her, and she waved back. She heard the strange whispering in the wind. "Lorelei is coming. Run fast." It gave her cold chills, but she stood her ground and stayed there watching Blake until his taillights were out of sight.

Nila and ran upon the front porch feeling an uneasy chill in the warm, summer air. She just couldn't shake the creepy feeling after hearing the whispering warning again. She felt she was being watched. Something ominous lurked in the dark.

Chapter 5

Nila turned the doorknob to her front door and walked in. "There's my Nila," her grandmother said as she gave Nila a hug and a kiss.

Nila returned the hug and kiss, "How was your visit with Aunt Kate?"

"It was good, but I missed you so much. Did your friend find you?"

"Yes, ma'am. Thank you for letting him know where I'd probably be."

"He seems like such a nice boy. But there's something familiar about him. I just can't put my finger on it. So what happened with Dawn today?" her grandmother asked with a sigh.

"Same old crap. She just got the best of me. I had to get away from her. Can you write me an excuse for tomorrow?"

"Sure can, darling. I'll just say you were sick, sick of Dawn Williams. How's that?" she laughed.

"Um, maybe not what made me sick, just that I was sick."

"Okay. Whatever you want," her grandmother said laughing as she walked toward the kitchen. "I'm fixing something special for you and your daddy since I've been gone a few days. I know y'all haven't eaten well," she said as she poured thick, yellow, cornbread batter into a large, black iron skillet coated with hot, sizzling butter.

Nila watched her grandmother in admiration as she picked up the skillet with her apron wrapped around her hands, protecting her from the hot handle, and slid the skillet into the hot oven. Nila looked at her grandmother's hands with much sadness in her heart, how old and wrinkled they were—the age spots, burns, and scars from a lifetime of hard work.

Her grandmother always recited the old quote, "a woman toils from dusk to dawn and yet her work was never done." Nila thought this must be true for her grandmother. Her grandmother was always the first up and the last to go to bed. Nila took a long look at her from head to toe. She wondered how time could be so cruel to people. Nila had seen many pictures of Ruth at all ages of her life and remembered one in particular of Ruth when she was Nila's age. How beautiful she was, how much she resembled Nila. But she had changed so much over the years. She hadn't aged badly, but she had aged.

Nila's grandmother was a short woman. Not fat, but she had a little potbelly. Even though she was wrinkled, she wore her age well; after all, she was 71 years old and had 12 children, Nila's father being the youngest. Her grandmother's eyes were green—a faded green. She didn't wear glasses, and she had all of her own teeth. Her hair was gray, almost completely white, and she always kept it pulled back in a bun. Nila greatly admired her grandmother and appreciated the hard life that she had lived. She always treated her grandmother with great respect and always helped her with the housework.

Nila's grandmother had been teaching Nila how to cook since she was four. Ruth Jones had taught Nila many things, traditional southern crafts, like soap making, canning food, quilting, and such. She also taught Nila how to garden and how to put up food from the garden. She taught her other things, things of a supernatural nature.

Ruth was a believer in God but not organized religion. She said that man had corrupted the church, and she would have no part of their hypocrisy. She taught Nila the Bible but explained to her that there was more than just God and the Bible. She taught Nila the old Celtic ways as well. Ruth had taught Nila that all religions were somewhat tied together, and man had separated them for their own selfish purposes.

Nila's grandmother taught Nila about how some spirits needed help to cross over and how they could help them. She taught Nila about angels, demons, and reincarnation. Ruth Jones had a special recipe book that was filled with ancient recipes that had been passed down through the family for centuries. It had recipes for healing herbs, rituals, and such. She taught Nila the importance of respecting nature and giving back when they take something. She always asked trees if she could have their leaves or bark, flowers if she could have petals or roots, and the river for its water.

She would give something back like a piece of bread, planting another plant, a gemstone, etc. Her grandmother would find strange little items while simply walking around in her everyday life, and she would give a verbal thanks to whatever left the gift for her. The first thing that Nila remembered seeing her grandmother find was a beautiful, little, blue jay feather laying at the front porch when Nila was five years old. Ruth Jones bent down, carefully picked up the feather, and tucked it away in her apron pocket to put away in a safe, special place later. She looked up into a nearby tree where there was a nest of blue jays and said, "Thank you, Mr. Blue Jay, for your lovely feather. I will take very good care of it." Then Ruth went into the kitchen and returned with a handful of cake and sprinkled it at the base of the tree. Nila asked her grandmother what she was doing. Her grandmother explained to Nila about the balance of nature and the importance of give and take.

Ruth also taught Nila the importance of not wasting. She never threw food in the trash. Instead, she would toss it out in the yard for the animals to use and let mother earth have the rest. She would even throw hair from the hairbrush in the yard for the birds to use in their nests.

Nila loved this about her grandmother. She also found herself absentmindedly doing the same things that her grandmother did. And that was okay with Nila. She was extremely proud to be like her grandmother.

"Nila, dear. Can you please clean those young onions over there in the sink?" her grandmother asked as she nodded her head in the direction of freshly picked onions with mounds of dirt still caked on them.

"Sure. The beans really smell good," Nila complimented her grandmother while taking in the wonderful scent of the brown beans simmering on the back stove eye.

"Thank you, dear. They've been cooking all day," her grandmother replied.

"Where's Dad?" Nila asked, as she glanced through the doorway into the living room at the indentation in the couch from the many evenings her dad relaxed there.

"He's upstairs washing up. He fixed your tire. He said you just about wrecked trying to miss a cat."

"It wasn't that bad. I just swerved to miss a cat and busted a tire, that's all. Speaking of cats, where's Lilly?" Nila asked, remembering that she hadn't seen her cat before she left for school that morning. Lilly was a beautiful black cat with a white splash across the top of her head. She had come to Nila the day Nila's mother died. No one knew where she came from. She just showed up on the doorstep and made herself at home. Since she was such a comfort to Nila, her father let her keep Lilly.

Ruth said that Lilly was an important part of Nila's life since she came to Nila in a time of great need. She also swore that Lilly was Nila's familiar, an animal sent to protect and guide someone with great spiritual abilities. Ruth believed that Nila had special gifts that hadn't yet matured. She believed that Nila's mother, Mary, had sent Lilly to her. So that day when Nila lost her mother, Lilly gained a family.

"She was up in your bed earlier waiting on you," her grandmother said as she pointed an old wooden spoon she had stirred the brown beans with in the direction of the stairs.

"I left in such a hurry this morning I didn't have time to look for her, and she didn't sleep with me last night."

"Girl, did you oversleep?"

"Yeah. I had problems sleeping," Nila confessed.

"Nila, do you need to talk to someone. You haven't been yourself lately. You've been a bit scatter-brained."

"Gee thanks, Grandma," Nila sighed.

"I've told you all your life that you're special. You have an old soul and you're meant to be great. But you need to let someone in and talk about what's bothering you. You know that boy, Kevin, his granny is a seer. She has helped many people over the years here in Legacy. She could really help you. Nila, maybe you should talk to her," Nila's grandmother suggested.

"Maybe I will. You're the second person to suggest that today. Kevin actually suggested the same thing."

"So you're telling some boy your problems but not your poor, old grandmother who loves you more than anything and has only cared for you since you were a baby," Ruth said playing the pity card. She knew that she could tug at Nila's heart this way and get her to tell her anything.

"Alright, Grandma. But it's a little embarrassing. I really don't want Dad to know. Okay?"

"Okay. He's a man and he doesn't need to know about women talk. To be honest, I don't think he wants to know about our women talk anyway," Ruth said as she picked up a fork and began to mash boiled potatoes in a bowl. Nila told Ruth in not so much detail about her dreams. She then disclosed the fact that the new boy Blake looked exactly like the boy from her dreams. How they made an instant connection. She told her about the weird whispering wind. By the time Nila had finished explaining everything to her grandmother, she had finished cleaning the young onions and was throwing the scraps out the kitchen door into the yard. She looked over at her grandmother to see a strange look upon her face. When Nila questioned her, she just said, "I knew something supernatural was going on with you."

"Grandma, what do you think is going on?" Nila asked.

"I'll have to refresh my memory and go through some old family archives to see for sure. There are many prophecies in our bloodline. Many have already come to pass and more are in the future to come. My best guess is that this is reincarnation. You and this boy Blake were together in a previous life. Maybe he has been dreaming about you. Maybe that's why he came here to Legacy," Ruth said trying not to look too concerned. But Nila could always tell when there was more than her grandmother was telling her. Ruth said it was a gift, but it wasn't one that she particularly liked when she didn't want to disclose everything to Nila, when she was trying to protect her.

"What do I do?" Nila asked as she heard her father's footsteps coming down the old, creaky stairs. "You won't mention this to Dad yet, will you?" Nila asked her grandmother with pleading eyes.

"Of course not. The men in this family don't always understand things like this. No use in worrying him about anything unless we know for sure there's something to worry about," Ruth said in a comforting and reassuring voice, letting Nila know that she could trust her grandmother above everyone else. She knew that her grandmother would always look out for her.

"Hey, Pumpkin," Nila's father said as he leaned over and kissed her on the top of the head. "Nila, you been at the lake? Your hair is damp and you smell like the lake."

"Yeah, I kind of skipped halfway through the day," Nila confessed.

"Just get bored?" he asked.

"Well, not really. I had a little too much Dawn Gale Williams. I just had to get away."

"What? Did you walk?"

"No," she said laughing. "Sherry and Kevin skipped with me."

"Well, just try to make it through the whole day tomorrow. Okay?" he said as he smiled and sat down at the table.

"Sure thing, Dad," Nila replied noticing how tired he looked. He looked older than what he actually was. David Jones had light brown hair and tanned skin; he was tall and thin. He had a small mustache. His eyes were green like Nila's and Ruth's. Nila noticed even as a child that when her mother had died her father aged markedly. When her mother had died, a part of her father had died as well. He had not been the same and never even gave another woman a second look. Nila always felt so bad for Dad, knowing how much he loved Mom and knowing that they were soul mates.

"I got your tire fixed. Now don't go running off the road to miss any more cats. Okay?" he snickered.

"Okay," Nila grinned as she helped her grandmother take the food to the table.

The three sat there and had a pleasant meal with small talk and laughter. Nila loved her father, grandmother, and Lilly. She really enjoyed her time at home with them. After dinner was over, Nila helped her grandmother clear the table and wash the dishes while her father watched television. When she finished helping her grandmother in the kitchen, she went into the living room and snuggled up with her father like a little child. He put his arm around her, and they watched television together while Ruth stitched together some pieces of cloth cut from old clothing to make a quilt top. Nila's mind kept wandering to Blake, the dreams, and the whispers. She finally gave up trying to watch television because she couldn't keep her mind clear.

"I'm going to bed now. I'm tired from swimming. I love you. And thanks for fixing my tire," Nila said to her father as she leaned over to give him a hug and kiss.

"I love you, Nila. Sleep well," David Jones said as he gave his daughter a hug and a kiss on the forehead.

"Thanks, Dad." Nila leaned over to give her grandmother a kiss and hug. "Goodnight, Grandma. I love you."

"Goodnight, dear. I love you," Ruth Jones said, giving her granddaughter a hug and a kiss.

Nila walked slowly up the creaky staircase to her bedroom. She walked into her dark room lit only by the shimmering moonlight that was spilling through her open window. But even in the dark room, she could see Lilly lying at the foot of her bed curled up fast asleep. Nila lay down on the old wrought-iron bed beside Lilly. "Hey, Lilly. Where were you this morning? I missed you today," Nila said as she stroked the cat from head to tail. Lilly rolled her sleepy eyes toward Nila, yawned, and stretched. She then meowed, purred, and rubbed all over Nila, letting Nila know that she missed her, too.

Lilly kissed Nila's face and sniffed her hair, wanting to know exactly where Nila had been all day. Lilly obviously smelled the water, grass, trees, and every other scent from the lake that was on Nila. After a few minutes with Lilly, Nila went to the bathroom to take a long, hot bath to wash the day off. Lilly followed Nila into the bathroom and found herself a cool spot in the floor next to the sink. Nila took off her clothes only to realize that she had left her wet underwear in Blake's car. She tossed her blouse and skirt onto the floor next to Lilly. She ran the water in the old claw-foot tub as hot as she could stand it. She stepped in slowly with the steam rising into the air, fogging up the mirror and the window.

Nila lay back in the tub, submerging her entire body in the water. As she rose from the water to a sitting position, she noticed Lilly washing herself. Nila just smiled and thought about the first time that she ever saw Lilly. She thought to herself, *I really love that cat. She makes me feel so good. She always knows how to comfort me. She always has.* Nila soaped up a washcloth with some of Ruth's homemade, lavender lye soap. It didn't lather well, but it smelled awesome. Nila washed while thinking of Blake. She couldn't wait to see him the next morning. She wondered if she would be able to sleep at all. She wondered if the dreams would yield any information that would help her make sense of it all. After Nila washed and rinsed, she lay back in the warm water to relax and fell asleep.

And the dreams came again.

Chapter 6

Nila couldn't believe it. She was back in the thicket, desperately searching for Blake. "Blake," she whispered, "Are you out here?" There was no response. It was just dark, lit only by sparse moonlight streaming through the trees onto the forest floor. Nila heard crickets, owls, wolves, and the rustling leaves in the trees from the wind. All of this was so familiar to her.

Nila began to wander around trying to find Blake. The forest scents were known to her—the scent of sweet dew lying atop the grass and leaves, the scent of sweet flowers, and even the scent of a distant lake. The warm, summer breeze lightly caressed her face and bare shoulders. She noticed her attire. She was wearing the same period clothing that she had worn in her other dreams. Nila grew frantic. She didn't like being alone in the dark forest. She was anxious to find her nobleman.

"Blake, are you here?" Nila called out as she tripped on a broken limb. She fell and scraped her hands and arms on a large maple tree as she tried to catch herself. The tail and bodice of her dress tore. She was so distraught and frightened that she just lay there where she had fallen. Nila wept as she heard something in the thicket quickly approaching. She was afraid to move for fear that whomever or whatever it was would surely hear her. If she didn't make a sound, she thought that they or it would perhaps pass her by.

The rustling on the forest floor got closer to where she lay. She felt like a frightened animal caught in a trap. Frozen in fear, she felt a cold hand fall upon her bare shoulder. Her heart sank when she turned to find the very same soldier her beloved nobleman had been battling the night before. His appearance was hideous with deviant, dark, evil eyes; dirty, dark, shoulder-length hair; rotten teeth; and a putrid smell emanating from every part of his disgusting body. Nila longed to awaken from her dream but to no avail.

"Got you!" the disgusting, depraved soldier exclaimed while trying to get a better grip on Nila by grabbing her with his other hand as well. He knelt down with his knees on the outside of her legs, pinning her down with her own dress. The soldier took Nila's hands with one of his and held them above her head, crushing them against the tree she had scraped herself on just moments earlier. He leaned in to kiss her; she struggled against him. His kiss was not like Blake's. Instead, it was harsh and cruel and left Nila's lower lip bleeding.

Nila cried out and furtively struggled to free herself from his grasp. The soldier pressed his dirty hand firmly against Nila's mouth, stifling her terrified screams. "Ah. No, no, no. We'll have none of that. Miss Lorelei made it perfectly clear that it did not matter if you were presented to her dead or alive. I can easily present you dead, if you like. Or you can behave yourself," he growled in her ear through stinking, gritted teeth.

Nila's eyes welled with tears, certain that her fate was sealed. She closed her eyes tightly and braced herself for the worse. Then the soldier's stinking, heavy body fell upon her, completely crushing her until she couldn't breath. She was shocked into opening her eyes and was surprised to see why he had fallen so heavily upon her body, smothering her beneath him.

Blake was retracting his sword from the dirty soldier's back. Blake pushed him over off of Nila with his foot, reached down, and grabbed Nila's hands, helping her to her feet. "Come on, we must go quickly." Nila asked no questions. She followed him as fast as she could. The sound of dogs barking and other soldiers' voices grew faint in the distance behind them. She assumed they were successfully treading in the opposite direction. Nila was still sobbing; it was hard for her see in the dark forest through tearing eyes. Yet, she held furiously to Blake's hand and ran far and fast. After about 30 minutes, Blake slowed to a walk and led Nila into a cave. The cave entrance was almost undetectable. If she had not been led there by Blake, she would not have noticed it at all.

Blake pulled her in closely and held her tightly. Nila felt liberated as she let herself go and sobbed uncontrollably. He didn't say a word but held her gently and lovingly, letting her know that he loved her more than anything.

Finally, when Nila was able to control her tears, Blake pulled back away from her and asked, "Nila, are you okay? Did he hurt you? Was I too late? What are you doing out here?"

Nila tried to respond completely and clearly to all of Blake's questions. "I'm fine, really. He didn't hurt me. You made it just in time. How did you know where I was?"

Blake responded, "I felt you were in trouble. I felt you reaching out to me, pulling me. I just let my heart and soul lead me to you. The important thing is that you are safe. You know they will eventually find us. She won't give up until they have."

"Who, Lorelei?" Nila guessed.

"Yes, of course. Who else? What's wrong with you?"

Nila was hit with the realization of what was happening. She wasn't dreaming. This was real. She had been traveling back into the past—her past life. Her grandmother had taught her a little about this type of thing. Nila remembered that Ruth had called it astral travel. Ruth told Nila that it was where the physical body stayed where it was supposed to be, but the spirit traveled to another place, time, or both. This was all that she knew about the phenomenon. She had no idea how to get back to where she belonged or how to keep from traveling back to her past life again. Nila knew that Blake must be what kept drawing her back.

"Here, come sit," Blake said as he handed her a cup of wine. Nila graciously took it from him and drank it quickly. She was parched from all of the running. He handed her an apple and a piece of bread and sat her down on cushions and blankets that were spread on the floor of the cave near a warm, bright fire that Blake had left burning. He carefully removed her boots and finished tearing her very ripped dress that left it just above the knee. He used the cleanest parts of the cloth of the dress to dip into a nearby bucket of water perched on a large, flat boulder. He carefully and gently cleaned her cuts and scratches. Then he used the remainder of the cleanest pieces of cloth to dress her wounds. As Blake cared for Nila's wounds, Nila ate her apple and bread, wincing intermittently from sudden pain.

When Blake had finished caring for her wounds, he sat beside Nila and pleaded with kind and concerned eyes, "Now, Nila, why are you here?" Blake said.

Nila thought to herself, *These are the eyes of a lover—a soul mate. He has the eyes of the loveliest person in the world. He surely must love me. I think he would give his life for me. I wonder if the Blake in my time feels the same.* After a moment, Nila snapped back and replied, "Really, I don't know." Nila told Blake everything, leaving no detail out of her story. She explained to him about her dreams, her future life, her family and friends, her Blake, and the whispering wind. As she moved deeper into her story, Blake's concern changed to fear. A lone tear run down his face. Nila wasn't even sure at first of what she saw because the firelight was so dim, but then she saw Blake reach up and quickly wipe the tear away. "What is it?" she queried, as she reached up to touch his face.

Blake solemnly responded, "This means that the sorceress, Lorelei, will find you and kill you—that the prophecy will come to pass."

"Okay, this is all very disturbing, but there's something I need to know before we go any further," she declared. "I want to know the whole sordid story about where we are, what year it is, why we are forbidden to be together, and why Lorelei wants me dead. First, I need to know if your name is Blake, and how do you know that my name is Nila?"

"Yes, my name is Blake, Blake Billings. I know that your name is Nila Anne Jones, because we are betrothed. I have loved you since the day I met you," he replied in a confused state.

At that moment, Nila knew that she was in the body of the ancestor she was named for. She also realized that in this time period she would die soon, since her ancestor had died very young. Nila wished she had studied her family tree a bit closer. She didn't know exactly when her ancestor, Nila Jones, had died, only that she had died very young. Nila was eager to get back to her grandmother so she could find out everything she could about the other Nila Anne Jones. Lost in thought, Nila had neglected to respond to Blake.

"Nila, are you alright?" Blake asked as he took her hands in his. His hands felt warm and gentle. Even though Nila was very frightened, she couldn't help but feel excitement growing within her. She thought that Blake felt the same as she did because of the way he touched her hands and looked into her eyes.

"I'm fine. I want to know everything but not right now. I need a few minutes to clear my head. Okay?" Nila said as she lay back among the plush cushions beside the fire. Blake lay down beside her and gazed into her eyes. He was amazed at how beautiful she looked by the firelight with the orange, flickering flames catching the green flecks in her eyes. He couldn't imagine living without her. He was fearful of the prophecy—terrified of being forced to live the rest of his life without her.

Nila's nobleman slid one arm under her back and cupped the back of her head with his hand, enjoying the feel of her soft hair intertwined in his fingers. Blake's body was partially atop hers, as he leaned in and brushed her soft lips with his until they were enthralled in a deep passionate kiss. Nila reached up and ran her fingers through his dark locks as she returned his exhilarating kiss. Nila and Blake were swept away by the waves of excitement of young love.

But as all the times before in Nila's dreams and at the lake, Blake stopped just short of total rapture. Nila didn't want him to stop touching her and kissing her. She loved the feeling of his skin against her; of his warm, sweet breath on her; the sweet, moist warmth of his kisses; and the hardness of his manhood pressing against her, letting her know how much he desired her. She longed for so much more. Blake whispered into Nila's ear, "The time is not perfect, not yet." Nila let go at that and just enjoyed the bliss of lying in her nobleman's arms with her head resting against his strong chest. Nila felt so comforted and at peace.

It was quiet except for the crackling fire, Blake's breathing, and the rhythmic beating of Blake's heart. Nila let herself drift into a deep sleep. She was awakened by a scratchy tongue licking her cheek. When she opened her eyes, Lilly hovered over her.

Nila was back where she belonged, back in her present life in her claw-foot tub full of cold water. Nila smiled and gave Lilly a wet pat on the head, but Lilly didn't mind. Nila stepped out of the old, porcelain bathtub and slowly dried off. As she ran the towel across her skin, she noticed scratches on her hands and knees. Then she ran her tongue across her lip where it had been bitten. It was sore and swollen. She felt sure she had actually traveled back in time.

Nila didn't take time to dress. She wrapped a dry towel around her and went to bed—anxious to get back to her noblemen. But no more dreams came. Nila was a bit disappointed when she awoke at the sound of her alarm clock. She opened her eyes to find Lilly snuggled up against her bare breasts. Lilly felt so warm and soft. Nila wondered if Lilly had slept like that all night. Nila hated to disturb her, she looked so peaceful. Nila quietly slid out of the bed, careful not to rouse the little, fuzzy, black cat—her special friend.

Nila took her time dressing and doing her hair and makeup. She wanted to make sure she looked immaculate when she saw Blake that day. She gave Lilly a hug and a kiss, grabbed her things, and went downstairs for breakfast. Her father had already left for work. She was greeted by her smiling grandmother.

"Good morning, Nila. Did you sleep well?"

"Well, yes and no," Nila replied, knowing that she needed to completely confide in her grandmother because of what she had discovered in her dream the night before.

"What do you mean, dear?" her grandmother questioned with concerned eyes.

"Well, I didn't have any dreams after I went to bed last night. So I slept very well from then on. But before I went to bed, I fell asleep in the bathtub and had a strange dream." Then she held out her hands to show her grandmother the bloody scratches. Nila explained how the scratches had occurred during her dream. "Grandma, do you think these are actually dreams or could it be astral travel?" Nila asked as she sat down at the kitchen table where a large cat-head biscuit smothered in gravy was waiting for her.

Ruth Jones didn't respond. She gingerly sat down at the table—kind of the same way she did the day she told Nila her mother had died. Her grandmother's action and lack of response terrified Nila.

"Grandma?" Nila said as she looked at Ruth Jones.

"Nila, you should probably come home right after school today. We really need to have a long talk."

Nila nodded her head yes and did not question Ruth Jones. She picked at her food in silence for a few minutes, told her grandmother goodbye, and left for school—apprehensive about what she was going to learn that evening.

Chapter 7

When Nila arrived at school, she saw Sherry all decked out in her usual trampy clothing and Kevin looking like a cowboy cuddled up together outside her locker. There was no sign of Blake. "Sherry, have you guys seen Blake this morning?" "No, not yet. Why? Did something happen when he took you home last night?"

"No. Well, not bad. He kissed me goodnight when he dropped me off. I thought everything was fine when he left," Nila's voice expressed an uncertainty in her tone.

"Maybe he's just late or doing something for his aunt," Kevin interjected.

"Yeah, you're probably right," Nila said trying to reassure herself aloud.

Nila and Sherry went into their homeroom when the bell rang and Kevin went to his. The day passed slowly.

Nila could think of nothing but Blake. She had no idea of how to reach him; she didn't know where he lived. Then there was the concern on Grandma's face at breakfast when Nila mentioned astral travel.

It came time for art class. This was supposed to be Nila's refuge. But that day it was her hell. Blake wasn't there. Dawn wasn't there either. Nila's mind imagined all sorts of things. *Was Blake with Dawn? Were they off somewhere together? What were they doing? Was their time together the night before just Blake having a little fun? Was Blake a player?*

Nila pretty much wasted the whole day at school by worrying. Nila's only productive accomplishment was apologizing to Mrs. Carver for not helping her on the murals the day before. She was desperately trying to distract herself, not to mention the fact that she also felt really guilty for skipping out on Mrs. Carver. So Nila worked on the murals during her art class and study hall.

When the day was done, Nila drove straight home, wasting no time. She had to know what was on her grandmother's mind. She parked her car in the driveway under the tree where she and her mother used to picnic. Nila sat in the car reminiscing about that for a while when she noticed her grandmother looking out the living room window at her.

Nila got out of the car. As she approached the front porch, Ruth Jones came out carrying a tray holding two glasses, a bowl of sugar lumps, a bowl of lemon wedges, and a pitcher of sweet, iced tea. "Nila, come sit on this swing beside an old woman while she tells you a story." With a tremble in her hands, Ruth sat the tray down on a nearby white, wicker table. Whatever her grandmother had to tell her must be extremely important by the serious look on her face, her quivering hands, and the care she had taken in preparing the tray.

"What kind of story, Grandma?" Nila questioned as she timidly approached the old porch swing and sat.

"Well, dear, it's hard to put in just one category. You see, it's not yet finished either. It's a story that's been in the making, oh, I don't know, about 500 years," Ruth said as she sat beside Nila on the old swing.

"Wow, a story that has been in the making for 500 years! I'd like to meet the author," Nila said with a little giggle, trying to lighten the mood.

"Well, Nila, there have been many authors, and I believe you are one of them. I believe you will be the author who will write the ending," Ruth declared.

"Grandma, I am beginning to get frightened about all that has been happening. To top it off, Blake didn't show up for school today. I don't know how to contact him. I don't even know where he lives. I've never been disrespectful or rude to you and I'm not now, I swear. I just–. I just want you to tell me what's going on. Can you help me?" Nila cried out as tears began to grace her beautiful, green eyes.

Ruth put her arm around Nila and said, "Girl, don't get upset. I'm going to tell you all that I know. I'm sure Blake is fine. He's not going to leave your side, I can guarantee you that. Just sit here, have a glass of good old, sweet iced tea; dry your eyes; and listen."

Nila nodded for fear if she spoke she would burst into hysterics. Ruth started to tell Nila an old Celtic story that began about 500 years ago in Ireland where the Jones' family originated.

"The Jones women in this bloodline are very special. They have always been. About 500 years ago in Ireland, there were two Jones sisters who were famous in their village for their future sight and healing powers. When someone was sick or crops were failing, the village came to the sisters for help. They always helped and never asked for anything in return for using their gifts to help others. They believed that good karma was all the payment they needed."

"The village people helped the sisters in every way they could, because the sisters were so generous and kind-hearted. The men of the village would cut and bring firewood to the sisters and help with repairs around their cottage. The women would bring spun wool, fresh milk and eggs, and fruits and vegetables. The sisters never asked for anything but always graciously accepted. They would not let anything go to waste. If they had more than they could use, they gave any excess to ones in need."

"It was said that the sisters communicated with spirits, and that's how they knew what would come to pass. One afternoon, the sisters were taking a walk through the woods close to their cottage when they encountered a spirit of one of their ancestors who shared a prophecy with them that would come to pass 200 years in the future. However, there were two different endings to this prophecy—one good and one bad. If the prophecy 200 years from then ended badly, then in 300 more years it would come to pass as it should."

"The two women who were to be involved in this prophecy were descendents in the Jones' bloodline. Both women would be named Nila Anne Jones. The mothers, while pregnant, would be visited by the spirits of the sisters to let them know that these were the chosen children and their name should be Nila Anne Jones."

"The prophecy states that the first Nila would be a very powerful spiritual woman—a high priestess. There would be someone to help her fight and destroy an evil sorceress, Lorelei. It would be a boy of noble blood. He would fall in love with the beautiful peasant priestess and fight by her side."

"If the prophecy ended like it should, then the two young lovers, the priestess and the young nobleman, would defeat Lorelei and have a long and wonderful life together. Nila would do great good everywhere she went and to whomever she would encounter."

"However, if the prophecy took the negative direction, no matter what the young nobleman did, he would not be able to save his young lover from the sorceress. If this happened, the young nobleman was destined to kill himself so that he could join his beautiful peasant lover and be with her in spirit."

"The two young lovers would then be reborn and reunited 300 years from then to once again face Lorelei. Only this time, they would be armed with the wisdom from their past lives that would help them to defeat Lorelei once and for all."

"The young, peasant priestess would need great power, which would be inherited from the Jones bloodline, her noble lover, past knowledge, and spiritual guidance from her ancestors."

Ruth ended the story. "Nila, you are the reborn peasant priestess, Nila Anne Jones. I think you already know that. Your ancestors came to your mother when she was pregnant with you. The sisters told her that you were the second chosen child and that your name shall be Nila Anne. They also told her something that was not in the prophecy. Your mother shared this secret with me the night before you were born and she swore me to secrecy. She told no one else, not even your father."

"Mary told me that the sisters revealed to her that when you turned 5 years old, Lorelei would take her so that she couldn't guide and prepare you for your destiny. The sisters said that this had to happen because your mother wasn't to guide you in life but in death. They said that I should guide you in life. Mary should spiritually guide you. Your mother and the sisters will be by your side when you face Lorelei."

"You know your mother has never really left you. Her spirit stayed here. Some nights I pass by your room, and I swear that I can see Mary sitting on the side of your bed watching over you. Mary sent Lilly to give you comfort. Blake is your young nobleman. He was sent to protect you."

"There are a few things that I know for sure about the life and death of the Nila from the 1700s and some things that are still a mystery. I know that she was killed, and her body was burned atop a funeral pyre. Her ashes were gathered, kept safely, and handed down from generation to generation until now. I have her ashes hidden away. When the time is right, I will pass them on to you. The thing no one knows for sure is what happened to Nila's young nobleman. He disappeared after her death. No one ever found his body. They all just assumed that because of the prophecy, he went off somewhere secret and took his own life so that he could be with her once again." Ruth had disclosed everything she knew about the prophecy and things she that weren't in the prophecy and looked at Nila as if to say, *Any questions?*

Nila was stunned. She had no idea how to respond. "Grandma, how am I supposed to respond to this bomb that you just dropped on me? How am I supposed to react?

What do you expect me to say?" Nila's lovely, sea green eyes filled with tears—tears of fear and tears of sadness. Tears of fear because she did not want to meet the first Nila's fate. Tears of sadness over the loss of her mother and the two young lovers. These emotions she knew personally, and she was finding it difficult to stay composed.

"Nila, I know it's a lot to take in, but I have taught you so much throughout the years in order to carry out the wishes of your mother and prepare you for your destiny. I had hoped that you would come to know of the prophecy before it had to be told to you. I think that it would have been easier to hear and accept that way."

"Accept that I'm a Celtic priestess, reincarnated, and the target of an evil sorceress? How can I accept that?" Nila exclaimed through tears. But no matter how absurd all of this sounded, in Nila's heart, she knew that it was all true. It was true that Nila was of Celtic descent. She was named for an ancestor who had tragically died very young. Lilly had come to her the day her mother died. She had been having dreams about Blake long before he came to Legacy. And they had experienced an instant connection.

Ruth let Nila sit in silence, letting Nila take it all in. She put her hand on Nila's knee. Nila reached out and tightly grasped her grandmother's old withered hand. She used her free hand to wipe the tears from her eyes. She took a deep breath. She felt that her mother was close, which gave her some comfort. Then she heard whispers in her left ear, "My darling, Nila, I'm very proud of you. You have become such a beautiful person—inside and out. You know in your heart that you are the chosen one. You can fulfill your destiny. You will not have to do this alone. I will be with you, Grandma will be with you, the sisters will be with you, and, most importantly, Blake will be with you. I love you. Blessed be." Nila knew without a doubt this was her mother's voice. She immediately felt reassured and confident.

"Grandma, what do I do now?" Nila asked as she looked into her grandmother's old, wise eyes.

"I continue to teach you on the physical plane. You let your mother and the sisters in so they can teach you on the spiritual plane. Most importantly, you need to call that boy to you."

"I don't know how to find him," Nila contested.

"Not with your physical body. Use your heart and soul to call him."

"How?"

"Do you love him?"

"I only just met him. How can I know that I love him?"

"Nila, think beyond this physical world. Do you remember how you felt in the dreams or astral travel?"

"So you do think it was astral travel. I was projecting back in time into the first Nila's body."

"Yes, I do. Now answer my question. Tell me how you feel when you are with the nobleman in her time?"

"I feel like I would die for him and die without him. I feel like I don't really live unless he's near. I feel overwhelmed with joy and exhilaration when I am with him. When he touches me, I feel I only exist for him," Nila confessed.

"But do you love him?" her grandmother asked once again.

"Yes, I do."

"Then think of him. Let yourself be submerged in thought of him. Go wherever your thoughts lead you. Let your heart be your guide. Tell him you need him. Tell him to please come to you. Tell him you love him. Nila, make sure to think of the Blake you know today, not the past Blake. Okay?"

"I'll try."

"Nila, start with quiet meditation. Go somewhere quiet where you won't be disturbed. Okay?"

"Okay," Nila said as she stood up to go to her room.

"And, Nila."

"Yes, Grandma?"

"Give me that phone of yours," she said reaching her hand out to Nila. "Sherry Parker ain't going to help any if she calls just as you get a connection with Blake."

Nila smiled and handed over her phone. She turned and walked into the old farmhouse. Nila walked up the creaky stairs, listening carefully to every crackle of wood under her feet with each step that she took. She let her hand glide up the banister, feeling the cool smoothness of the wood. When she reached her room and walked in, she found Lilly lying on her bed curled up asleep. Nila picked up her little black companion, giving her a hug and a kiss as she explained to the cat how she needed to be alone for a while but she would find her when she was finished with her important task. She put the little cat down outside her bedroom door and said, "Sorry, Lilly ole girl." Lilly turned and flipped her tail in the air as if she were terribly insulted, took a few steps, stopped, turned, and gave Nila an insulted glance before prancing down the stairs. Nila closed the door and lay on her bed.

Nila closed her eyes and began to think of Blake. She thought of their time together at school, at the lake, and in his car. She thought about how good he smelled, how wonderful he looked, how his touch felt, and how he made her feel. Nila thought so intensely about Blake's scent that she could smell the musky, woodsy, scent of him as if he was standing beside her. She imagined his wavy, black hair and his beautiful, blue eyes that sparkled with the intensity of a star. Nila remembered how amazing the touch of his hand felt sliding across her leg and the warmth of his lips on hers. She thought about how euphoric he made her feel when he gazed intently into her eyes. She imaged him so intently that she believed if she opened her eyes he would be standing there.

Blake, where are you? I really need to see you. Please come to me. Your peasant priestess desperately needs you. Please come to me. Nila kept thinking this while holding the image of her young nobleman and letting that image dance through her mind. After about 30 minutes, as she was ready to give up, she heard a response in her head.

Blake's sweet voice whispered, *Nila, are you okay? I will be there soon. Don't worry. I'm on my way.*

Nila felt a little guilty because Blake sounded so distressed and worried. Nila simply answered, *Oh, thank you. I will be anxiously waiting.*

Nila opened her eyes not knowing whether or not to believe that what just happened had really happened or if it was all in her imagination. Had she just imagined it all? Had she and Blake really been communicating telepathically? If so, how?

Then there was a familiar feeling in her bedroom. It was her sweet, patient Lilly. Lilly jumped on the bed as if to say, *You're finished with your important task, now love me.* She snuggled in close as if to reassure Nila that everything would be just fine. "Lilly, how did you get in here?" Nila looked to see if the door was open. But it was still shut. Without any thought, Nila asked, "Mama, are you here? Did you let Lilly in? I really need some guidance. I can't do this without you. Yesterday, I was a normal girl going to school on the first day of my junior year. Tonight, I am a priestess who must defeat an evil sorceress. I don't know what to do. Please help me."

Little did Nila know that she had just tapped into her power as a spiritualist. Nila was surprised to see her mother standing before her. Mary Jones looked exactly the way she did the last time Nila saw her alive. Nila's mother wore a white cotton blouse and blue jeans with a pair of flip-flops on tan feet with pedicured toenails. Her long, black hair flowed liked a waterfall across her shoulders and down her back. She starred lovingly at Nila with doe-like eyes shining brightly. Her dark skin reminded Nila why she herself had dark skin and dark hair. Mary Jones was a Cherokee Indian. The only things that Nila inherited from her father's Irish ancestry were her green eyes and spiritual abilities. Other than her green eyes, one would think that Nila was a full-blooded Cherokee as well.

Mary eased forward so as not to frighten Nila, as she slowly reached out her hand for her daughter. Nila didn't know what to think. *Is she a ghost or is she in my imagination? It doesn't matter. Either way, I can't touch her.* But even in Nila's skepticism, she reached out for her mother's hand. Amazingly, Nila's fingertips touched Mary's hand. Nila was surprised that it was as solid and warm as her grandmother's hand had felt earlier on the front porch. Immediately and fluently, they embraced.

"Oh, Mama!" Nila cried out, thinking how strange those words sounded falling from her lips. Nila never thought she would hear these words coming from her mouth again. "Is it really you? How are you here? Do

Grandma and Dad know?" Nila quickly questioned not giving her mother time to respond in between questions.

"Yes, I'm really here. I came to help you because you conjured me. You brought me here with sheer will."

"How?"

"My darling, you are a great spiritualist or what the Cherokee call a shaman. You have not only received gifts from your father's powerful ancestors but mine as well. My grandfather was a shaman," Nila's mother began.

Nila had a myriad of questions and couldn't ask them quickly enough. "How did I not know all of this? Do Grandma and Dad know about this? Why haven't they told me?"

"Nila dear, calm down. Take a long breath, and let me explain. Yes, Grandma and Dad know. We wanted to give you all of this information slowly and over a long period of time. We had to wait until you were old enough to understand the great responsibilities that come with your great gifts. You must continue to be patient."

"How can I be patient when there is a crazy, powerful sorceress coming to kill me? I have heard warnings in the wind that sound almost like whispers."

"That was the sisters warning you. You must work long and hard with your grandmother. Don't ask so many questions. All will be revealed when the time is right. And Blake knows more than you and your grandma think he knows. Let him help guide you. He, too, will in time reveal much knowledge that will help you," her mother said reassuringly as she reached up and brushed a tear from Nila's cheek.

"What do I do right now?" Nila pleaded with her mother.

"You continue to let your grandmother guide you, and listen when the sisters call out to you. Today, you will enjoy time with Blake. He will be here soon. Just tell him everything you know. He will help fill in the blanks as the time is right. Don't push him for answers. Trust me on that. And trust Blake completely. After you share everything with Blake, enjoy your time with him. Yours and his is a lost love rediscovered. Don't be frightened of the strong feelings that you have for him. Embrace those feelings. And, Nila, ignore everything Dawn Williams does or says to you. Negative energies will only weaken you and hurt you in the long run. Focus on your family and Blake," Mary said as she began to fade like a scene from an old black-and-white movie—The ones that Nila loved so much.

"Momma, don't leave," Nila cried out.

"I have to, my darling girl, but I will return. I am always with you. You just can't see me. I will return in flesh soon. If you need me, really need me, just call to me again like today. I love you, Nila. Blessed be." She was gone like she had never even been there.

"Momma," Nila called out as she heard a knock at her bedroom door. Thinking it was her grandmother, she opened the door, eyes brimming with tears, and immediately fell into the arms of the person standing there. She was already committed to the embrace when she saw that it was Blake and not her grandmother. But it did not matter, this was much better.

Chapter 8

"Nila, are you okay? What's wrong?" Blake asked full of all the concern and fear of an old lover.

At that moment, Nila understood what her mother meant when she said that theirs was a lost love rediscovered and why she had told her to trust Blake completely. He truly loved her. She could see that in his eyes, hear it in his voice, and feel it in his embrace. But how? He only just met her. How could they have such strong feelings for one another when they just met? Nila understood that there was a connection because of the past life they had shared. She knew that she loved him and that her past self had intensely loved the past Blake. But how was he so certain of his love for her?

Nila asked Blake in. "Come on in, and I will try to explain it all. But it may take a while. You probably won't believe any of it. In fact, you may turn and run away and never look back again," she said between sobs.

Blake said not a word. He simply took Nila's hand in his and led her to the bed where they took a seat on the edge. "Nila, you can tell me anything. I will believe anything you tell me, and I will be there for you. I swear," Blake said as if he were declaring his undying love and loyalty to Nila.

Nila felt as if a huge boulder had been lifted from her body as Blake swore his oath to her. Through tear-filled eyes, she gazed into his deep blue eyes filled with love. "Okay, here it goes," Nila told her story as they sat on the bed hand-in-hand. It seemed like it took half the night to tell Blake everything. She confided in him about the dreams of him, the whispers of warnings about Lorelei that belonged to the sisters, about the prophecy, everything.

Blake smiled at Nila, took her in his arms, and gave her a long and loving embrace that Nila never wanted to end.

Because of Blake's lack of response, Nila was certain that he thought this was all a big joke or something. "Nila, I have known all of this for such a long time. You are the reason I came to Legacy. I thought that you already knew who I was. But you seemed so unsure of yourself, so I played along, trying to give you time to figure it all out," Blake confessed.

Blake looked as relieved as Nila felt. "How long have you known?" she asked.

"Pretty much most of my life. My parents were originally from Legacy. I knew of the prophecy, of you, and of the role I was to play in it. The prophecy isn't as secret as you may think. Your love drew me back here to you," Blake said with a huge smile that could surely light up a room in a pitch-dark cave. Blake leaned over and kissed her gently on the mouth.

His lips were so sweet and soft. Nila knew at that moment that they did truly love each other. Even though Nila had been dreaming about Blake for months and only known him for two days, it felt as though they had loved each other for centuries. She knew that they truly belonged together—that they were soul mates. All of her concerns that day about Blake being with Dawn completely disappeared.

Nila's room grew dim with the setting sun. She reached over and turned on a lamp her mother had given her for her fourth birthday. It gave the room a low illumination. Nila saw Blake as if for the first time. He knew her secrets, and she knew his. They loved each other, and they were eternally tied to one another. She totally trusted him. As she looked into his eyes, she could feel the pull of the universe drawing her deep into him. She knew that there was no place she ever wanted to be other than by his side. She knew that Blake felt the same.

Blake reached up and touched her face with such a soft and gentle caress that Nila likened it to a soft, warm, summer breeze grazing her skin.

Just as Nila and Blake had become lost in one another, she heard a soft knock at her door. Blake's hand dropped in reflex, and they both stared at the door as Nila said, "Come in."

"Dinner's ready," her grandmother said almost timidly, not sure of the state Nila was in. "Is your young gentleman, Mr. Blake, staying?" she asked Nila. Before Nila could respond, Ruth said to Blake. "You're more than welcome."

Caught off guard, Blake stammered a, "I don't–"

Before he could say *think so*, Nila interjected, "I would really like it if you would stay, if it's okay with your aunt and if you would like to stay."

"Well, okay then," Blake said, knowing that he could never deny any wish that he could grant Nila. "I'd love to," Blake continued, as he gazed deeply into those beautiful eyes that silently said *thank you.* He responded with the thought *you're welcome.*

Nila smiled, not realizing that she had sent that thought out to him. He smiled and reached over to take her hand.

Ruth knew they had made the connection. Thinking of her own husband when they were young and in love, she smiled at the young couple and said, "Well then, come on before it gets cold."

They walked together, holding hands, down the stairs. Nila thought to herself how different her trip down was from her journey up just a few hours before. How alone and scared she had felt earlier and how comforted and protected she now felt.

"Hello, Dad," she said, as she sat in the chair that Blake had pulled out for her and looked up at Blake and smiled. "This is Blake Billings. Blake this is my father," Nila introduced them to one another.

"Blake," David said as he reached out his right hand.

"Mr. Jones, it's so nice to meet you," Blake said as he shook David Jones' hand.

"Nila. I trust your day was better today," her father said as he dipped a large ladle of brown gravy and topped his mashed potatoes with it.

"Much better this evening, thank you."

"Nila, your grandmother and I had a talk this evening. I know I haven't been very expressive about your heritage and your gifts through the years, especially recently. It has traditionally been left up to the women of the Jones family to guide the daughters through this journey. It's obvious you know the Jones women in the family keep their maiden name when they marry and their children take the name Jones."

"Yes, sir," Nila stated. She had known this since childhood.

"Well, the reason is to keep the sacred name of Jones strong. This is what the witches believed, and so it has been for centuries. If this indeed gives strength to the Jones women, then you are more powerful than you can imagine. I think Blake here knows just how strong you are capable of being," David Jones said as his words went out first in Nila's direction, then to Blake as he raised his eyebrows.

Blake nodded and said, "Yes, sir."

And that was the end of that discussion. They continued the meal with small pleasantries and lovers' glances between Nila and Blake. When dinner was over, Blake got up to leave. After Blake bid farewell to Ruth and David Jones, he and Nila walked out to the front porch.

The couple embraced for a long time. Blake whispered into Nila's ear over and over that everything would be okay. "I'll not leave your side, ever." Then he whispered with his lips against her neck, with his warm breath searing her skin, "I love you, Nila Jones. I have for so many years." Nila had no clue of just how long Blake had loved her.

"I love you Blake Billings, responded Nila, surprised by her ready reply that came forth without thought. The words felt familiar and natural.

He pulled her in closer and tighter, until their bodies melded. He stroked her soft hair and buried his face deep into the hollow of her neck, taking in her sweet unique scent—a combination of lavender and honeysuckle. They stood there like that for what seemed like forever.

Blake finally broke the embrace and told Nila he should go so his aunt wouldn't worry. "I'll see you in the morning. I love you, Nila Jones."

"I can't wait. I love you, Blake Billings," Nila replied.

Nila watched as Blake descended the steps of the front porch and walked to his car. She watched as he drove out of sight, until she no longer see the taillights of his car. She turned slowly with dreamy eyes and a permanent smile on her face and walked into the house that had been her home since birth.

Waiting for Nila just inside the front door with her arms crossed and something in her right hand that was barely visible from under her left elbow, Ruth said seriously, "Nila, we need to talk about that boy."

Chapter 9

"Come sit, child. Look what I found in an old family heirloom trunk in the attic. So that I could give you some time undisturbed, I went to look through old papers to see if I could find more information about the sisters and the prophecy for you. I ran across this. It was actually on top of a stack of handwritten books," she explained as she reluctantly handed the piece of paper to Nila. "I knew that boy looked familiar," Ruth Jones continued.

"What is it?" Nila asked as she looked at the piece of paper. It was a small sketch. It was signed Nila Anne Jones, and it was dated 1728. This wasn't her drawing. *It can't be!* Nila noticed how old and decrepit the paper looked and how fragile it felt between her fingertips. She just knew this was not one of her sketches. The paper was too old, withered, and stained. She would never let one her sketches come to be in this condition. She was in shock. Her voice shook as she said, "Grandma, this is Blake, but its dated 1728."

"I know. This is the first Nila Jones' beau. This boy was her lover; he was the one to be reincarnated with her. I don't understand why he looks exactly like Blake. The first Nila looked nothing like you. Here," she said as she handed a second sketch to Nila, this time shoving it at her anxiously, not reluctantly as she did with the first sketch. "This is the first Nila Jones."

Nila was astounded by the young woman's beauty. The woman in the drawing was the most beautiful girl Nila had ever seen before. She looked nothing like Nila. "Well, what does this mean?" Nila asked her grandmother.

"I'm not sure," Ruth Jones confessed.

"Grandma, I have to tell you something. When I was in my room earlier, just after I was able to contact Blake, Momma came to me."

Ruth looked puzzled as she asked with eyebrows furrowed, "What do you mean, came to you? Did you have a vision? Did you see her spirit?"

"Not exactly," Nila confessed. "I don't how I did it, but I was so upset that I just called out her name and told her that I really needed her. She just appeared to me—in the flesh. I was able to talk to her, hug her, and smell her. It was almost like she had never been gone. She told me that you would tell me all that you knew and that Blake would tell me everything else that I needed to know. But she said not to push him, that he would tell me what I needed to know when the time was right. She also told me that I should just trust him, totally."

"Then you have connected with the spirit world. Your momma knows so much more than you or I. My advice is to do what she says," Ruth Jones said as she reached out with open arms, inviting Nila in for a hug. "Alright, Nila girl, you best get some rest. It's been a long day."

"Okay," Nila said with her head buried in her grandmother's shoulder like a tiny child. Nila turned to her father who was sitting on the sofa not making a sound. She walked to him and said, "Daddy, I love you," leaning down and hugging him tightly, really appreciating the fact that she still had him.

David Jones reached up and hugged his daughter tightly and said with such sadness in his eyes, "Nila, you are about to have to face something that I cannot help you with. I feel so useless. But I do know in my heart that that boy is the one you must depend on."

Nila couldn't remember him looking this sad since her mother had passed away.

He continued, "I know this because Mary came to me last night, in flesh as well. I thought that I dreamed it, but now I know that she was real. She told me that Blake would be your savior, not me. That really hurt me, but I understand that this thing is bigger and older than I am. This story was written long ago. Who am I to try to change it? If she says he's the one to stand by you in your hour of need, then that's what must be done."

Nila felt so confident knowing that this boy she had fallen in love with before she ever met him was the same boy that her family was certain she should put her faith in and trust. She finished her goodnights and went upstairs to her bedroom. Lilly followed. Nila didn't turn on a light or close the door. She wanted a bath but was so tired that she couldn't muster up the courage or strength to walk to her bathroom. She fell back onto her bed, kicked off her shoes, shimmied out of her pants, and pulled her top across her head. Lilly jumped into bed and snuggled into Nila's hair. They fell asleep instantly.

It wasn't long before Nila was whisked to the past again. This time, there was no nobleman in sight. She was cold and alone in the dark. As her eyes adjusted to the darkness, she saw that she was in a dungeon. A woman laughed—not a laugh of joy but one of wickedness. The sinister noise belonged to the evil woman, Lorelei. "Well, well, you finally decided to join the land of the living. Don't worry, it won't be for long. I am still awaiting the hunters and the dogs tracking Blake. When I find him, I will finish you and take what's mine—him. He can never be made to want me until he sees that your love is no longer. The only way to do that is to kill you," the woman laughed as she turned and walked away, leaving Nila alone.

Nila's heart sank. She knew beyond the shadow of a doubt that this was the fate of the first Nila Jones. She knew that this was the end. Nila lay there on the cold, wet floor of the gloomy dungeon for what seemed like hours. Finally, she heard the unmistakable voice of her lover. Lorelei's henchmen tossed Blake into the cell beside her.

Blake looked distraught, sad, and humbled. "Nila, my love, I have failed to fulfill my oath to you. I have let you fall into harm's way and into the hands of Lorelei. My love, I will surely die if the prophecy holds true. I cannot go on without you. I will take your hand in death," Blake said, sobbing and shaking, tears streaming down his face.

Nila had to get through to Blake, to let him know that this was not the end. She reached up to the rusty bars of the cold, dirty cell and grasped his hands in her own. "Blake, please don't give up on me or us no matter what happens here tonight. You must find me again. You know the prophecy. If I die tonight, I will be reborn. Remember this, and find me. I swear that my love will draw you to me. Do not weep, my love, this is not the end. You know that to be true. This is a new beginning. I will fare well with my mothers and sisters on the astral plane." Nila leaned up and kissed her nobleman.

Nila's assuring kiss sent ripples of calm through Blake's body. Blake regained the confidence Nila was accustomed to in him. She felt much better, much stronger, and no longer fearful.

Lorelei and her guards bounded in to take Nila away, leaving Blake in panic and despair. He fell to his knees and cried, "Nila! Please, I will do anything you ask of me, just do not harm her!"

Lorelei threw her head back and cackled. She leaned close to Blake, inches from his face, and growled through her teeth, "There is nothing to be done for her." She spun back to Nila and wrapped a rope around her neck. One of Lorelei's brutes took the rope from her hand and yanked Nila to the floor, up the stairs, and out of the dungeon.

Nila felt the rope tightening around her neck, cutting off her air supply. Everything around her turned pitch black. Blake's screams and cries diminished in the background. Nila felt warm, kind hands and heard a sweet, loving whisper in her ear. "Nila, it's okay. That's all in the past, you're safe here. I won't let you down again. I swear. I love you, and I will not let anything happen to you this time. Wake up."

Nila opened her eyes to see Blake lying on his side with one arm under her neck and the other resting on her chest with his hand gently caressing her face. She felt so safe and secure with Blake holding her and comforting her. When she realized that she was in her underwear, it did not matter. Blake was her protector, and she trusted him completely. Nila reached up and embraced her nobleman. She whispered into his ear with such sweet tenderness, "I love you, my sweet nobleman."

He smiled, knowing that with those words spoken she was beginning to remember just how much she had once loved him in her past life. He whispered in her ear with the same tenderness, "I love you, my peasant priestess."

Nila was dazed from her dream. She wasn't sure if Blake was really there, even though she could feel his warm and gentle but strong embrace and see his deep blue eyes.

Blake instinctively knew what she was thinking. "I'm really here. You are really awake."

Nila smiled at the sound of his voice. She looked at him intently, savoring everything about him—his eyes, his hair, his touch, his smile, and his scent. Nila suddenly became aware of her morning breath, so she hastily reached over to the nightstand, grabbed a piece of spearmint gum, popped it into her mouth, and began to chew.

Blake smiled at her insecurities. *Someone so strong, yet so unsure of herself,* he thought. Blake leaned in and kissed her on the mouth while sill holding her in his arms. His passionate kiss sent chills down Nila's body.

Nila reached up and grabbed the back of Blake's head, wrapping her fingers around his loose, black waves, pulling him into her, kissing him back with such passion and intensity that Blake felt a surge of emotions that he had not allowed himself to feel in such a long time. He longed to act on his feelings—her feelings. He wanted to take her, but he knew that she wasn't ready, even though she thought she was. He pulled back after letting his hands explore her body during the kiss. "Nila, I'm so sorry," Blake apologized breathlessly.

"Sorry? Sorry for what? Please don't be sorry."

"I just don't think we should go any further, not just yet. There are so many things that I need to tell you first, so much you need to know before anything substantial happens, if you know what I mean," he stammered.

"You really are a gentleman, aren't you?" Nila replied. "So tell me what I need to know before we make that commitment to one another."

"Now? But we have school in a couple of hours."

"I can skip, how about you?" Nila asked.

"Stay here?" Blake asked puzzled.

"No, the lake."

"When?"

"I'll meet you there in about 45 minutes," Nila said smiling, thinking how easy it was to convince Blake to skip, meet her at the lake, and tell her what he thought she needed to know.

"Okay," Blake said as he leaned in and kissed her again, but not with as much passion as before. He didn't want to have to suppress those passionate emotions again so soon. Blake climbed out the window and down the trellis. And just as his foot touched the ground, he heard, "Good morning, Blake." It was the voice of Nila's grandmother, Ruth Jones.

Blake was embarrassed but slowly turned to Ruth and began to explain only to be interrupted by the old woman.

"There's no reason to explain anything about this," as she pointed to Nila's room. "I know that you come to her when she needs your protection."

But Blake felt the need to explain. He felt he owed that to Ruth. "Last night, she had the sight or vision of the first Nila's death. I knew she would need me when she awoke."

Ruth asked with her brows furrowed and head tilted to one side. "And have you had these visions of the first Nila's death too?"

"Well, kind of."

Ruth sat down on the porch swing and patted the seat beside her. "Come sit with me. I found something, and I need to ask you about it."

"Okay," Blake said, as he walked to the swing, wondering what could be so important by the serious look on Ruth's face and the sound in her voice.

Ruth drew the sketch from her apron pocket as Blake sat down beside her. Blake's face told Ruth that he knew all about that sketch. Ruth was surprised when she saw the expression on his face at the sight of the old and battered sketch.

Blake took the piece of paper from Ruth, fell onto the old woman's shoulder, and wept like a child. It was a sketch that Blake thought was gone forever.

"What is it, boy? You seen this before, have you?"

"Yes, ma'am," he said between sobs.

"Blake, I can barely understand you. Calm down. You are supposed to be Nila's protector. Collect yourself and tell me what you know about this picture," Ruth said as she lifted her old and wrinkled hands to steady him with a force he wasn't prepared for, lifting him off her shoulder to face him.

"I thought this was destroyed by Lorelei. How did you come by it?"

"I found it in an old, family heirloom trunk in the attic yesterday. Who drew it, and why does this Blake look exactly like you when the first Nila and my Nila look totally different?"

Just as Blake began to explain, Nila bolted through the front screen door and onto the front porch. She didn't know what to think when she saw Blake and her grandmother sitting on the front porch swing together,

Blake holding that sketch with tears streaming down his face.

Blake looked up at Nila and motioned her over to him. "This was something that I was going to tell Nila today. But I guess I should explain it to you both now," he began. "This is a sketch of me in 1728. The first Nila was an artist just like you," he said, as he looked at Nila. "She sketched me whenever she had the chance. This was the last sketch that she did."

Nila and Ruth's jaws dropped open. "What do you mean, of you?" Nila asked, barely able to form the words.

Blake replied, "I have not been reincarnated like you. I have been waiting on you all these years, never growing a day older."

"How is that possible?" Ruth asked.

"After Lorelei killed Nila and unsuccessfully tried to bed me, I was able to escape with the help of a chambermaid who had known and loved Nila as a sister. Lorelei had betrayed many, including witches and wizards—she did not discriminate on betrayal. One of those wizards found me—sick, cold, and half-starved in the woods, hiding from Lorelei. He knew that he was not powerful enough to exact his pound of flesh from Lorelei, but he knew of the prophecy. He knew that Nila could exact revenge for everyone."

Blake continued, "The old wizard didn't want to risk us not finding each other after reincarnation, so he made me immortal. In return, we were to destroy Lorelei. Then, it would be our choice to let Nila become immortal or me to once again be mortal. I had to disappear so that Lorelei would think that I was dead. The wizard told me that I would find you when you began to dream about me, of us, of our past. He said that I would share your dreams and that your love would draw me to you. He assured me that you would be reborn here in Legacy to the same family line. He said that you would be sent back here to Legacy where we once shared an undying love. And you know most of the rest."

Nila and Ruth sat in amazement, not knowing what to say, what to do, or what to think. Eventually, Nila turned to her grandmother and said, "Grandma, I need to skip today. I need Blake to tell me everything. I'll be back as soon as I can, and you can begin to teach me everything that you need to. Please."

"Of course. Nila, you are being prepared to take on something greater than anyone in Legacy can imagine. I think you should be able to have today to yourself. Take your time, and come back when you're ready. I won't worry. I know that you are in good hands," Ruth said. Then she hugged and kissed both Nila and Blake.

The couple descended the porch and walked down the road to Blake's car. Ruth walked into the house to try to go on with her day as usual, pondering what was to come.

Chapter 10

Before Nila knew it, she and Blake were at the lake lying on a blanket. Nila was so anxious to hear everything about the first Nila and Blake. But she could see how Blake was still upset. She didn't want to force him. She rolled over and positioned her soft breasts against Blake's chest. Her face was over his, and her hair brushed his head and neck.

Blake loved the feeling of Nila's hair falling loosely about him. It brought back memories of the first Nila. Even though the modern day Nila looked nothing like her ancestor, Blake could tell they shared the same soul. He couldn't distinguish between the two. It was as if they were one person merged together. Even more so now that Nila was beginning to remember more about her past life through her dreams. Blake knew that the time was right to tell Nila everything. He knew in his heart beyond a shadow of a doubt that she was ready. Blake looked deep into Nila's lovely green eyes and said, "Nila, I'm ready to help you remember. I feel sure that between what I tell you and the dreams you've had that everything will fall into place and you will remember you life as the first Nila Anne Jones and the time that we shared."

So Blake began his story—with his first encounter with Nila Anne Jones, reminiscing with a smile on his face and a twinkle in his handsome blue eyes at the memory of her. "It began in the year 1726. I was 15 and so was she. I was a young nobleman, and she was a beautiful peasant. It was an enchanting summer afternoon. I was riding my horse through the woods by this very lake. I had been on an errand for my father. I came this way because I wanted to water and rest my horse."

"There she was—bathing in the lake. All I could see were her shoulders and head. Every other part of her was submerged in the warm, summer water. The sun was shining on her beautiful, long, wavy, auburn locks that spilled across her shoulders and back and glistened against her alabaster skin. She turned to me. Her green eyes pierced my soul, inviting me into her own. I knew that when our eyes met that her soul was the missing half of my own."

"I thought she would run away in fear. She did not. Instead, she smiled a smile that would light up the night sky and introduced herself. I told her what my name was and apologized for looking. But I was honest with her and told her that her beauty bewitched me, keeping me from being able to avert my eyes no matter how hard I tried. She laughed and said that she was flattered."

"I had heard of her and her family and had only seen her once from a distance as a child. She now looked nothing like she did when I had seen her before, so much so that I was unaware of who she was when I introduced myself."

"Nila did not bow at my feet as other peasants did when I introduced myself as a nobleman. Instead, she walked proudly from the lake like a goddess emerging from a temple, beads of water kissing her beautiful, white skin as the sun illuminated it like tiny stars until she almost glowed. And there, resting atop of her breasts, catching the sunrays as if it were somehow connected to the sun, was a golden, Celtic knot pendent. I was surprised by her boldness. Nila did not hide her nakedness from me but proudly wore it like new clothing. She walked to me, slightly bowed to show respect, and reached her hand out to me. I took her silky, wet hand in my own, shuttering at the electricity that flowed between us. I held her hand up to my mouth and kissed it. It was by far the sweetest thing that had ever touched my lips. Nila looked up and smiled, 'It is a pleasure to meet you Blake Billings.'"

"She withdrew her hand, turned, picked up her clothes, and walked into the woods, looking back once over her shoulder and smiling at me. Nila melted my heart that day. I knew then and that I had to have her. I gave chase to her for a few months while she played the game of hard-to-get. Eventually, she admitted that she felt the same for me as I did for her."

"Normally, a nobleman and a peasant girl would have been forbidden to be friends, let alone lovers. But it was different with Nila. Her ancestors were wise and great witches and highly revered in their day—so it was throughout the years and so it was with Nila. Her family was held in high regard because they never took, they only gave. They never wasted or betrayed anyone, were always kind-hearted to friends and foe alike, and they did much for their neighbors. Even though Nila was but 15, she was more powerful than any of her kin before her. She was held highly by everyone who knew her, including my parents. This is why we were allowed to be together."

Nila imagined the things that Blake was telling her. She thought it was so strange how vivid these images were. It was almost as if she were remembering events from her own past. It wasn't her memories though, it was the memories of her ancestor invading her mind. Nila listened intently to Blake as he told the story of their past and she subconsciously played with the golden, Celtic knot pendent that lay loosely between her breasts.

Blake continued, "We had been together for two years. We were both now 17 and the year was 1728. It was early in the year; I believe it was January. My mother had fallen very ill with what is known today as pneumonia. It was common to die from this in that day. Nila concocted herbal remedies and stayed with my mother day and night, never leaving her side for two weeks. Everyone knew that my mother's death was inevitable. We had already prepared the arrangements associated with my mother's passing and said our farewells. No one would blame Nila if her remedies failed. We all knew that she had done everything that she could."

"Then one night I went to my mother's chambers to tell her goodnight. I knew by the hollow, distant look in her eyes that I would not be telling her good morning. I did not cry in front of her, but as soon as the chamber door closed behind me, I wept like a child. Nila heard my weeping and came to me. She embraced me tightly and whispered to me, 'Have you lost faith in me as everyone else has?' I told her no, I had not lost faith in her. I did not believe God himself could cure my mother. Nila asked for a few of my tears. I did not ask why, I only obliged her request. She gathered a few in a small, glass vial and bid me goodnight. She told me to sleep well and come to my mother's chambers at dawn. Then she closed and bolted the door from within. I went to my chambers but could not sleep."

"At dawn, I did not take the time to dress. Still in my nightshirt, I went to my mother's chambers. I knocked lightly on the door. I heard the loud clicking of the bolt unlatch. The door opened slowly with an eerie creaking. Nila was behind the door, clinging to it as if not to fall. She looked so pale and weak. She looked as if her soul had been ripped from her body. I knew that from the way she looked that she desperately tried and gave her entire self to try to save my mother. But I knew in my heart that she had failed."

"I walked to my mother's bed to find her eyes closed and her body lying still. I was certain that she had passed in the night. I knelt by her bedside, laid my head upon her bosom, and freely wept. A hand caressed the back of my head, but Nila was still clinging to the door. I raised my head to see who else was in the room. To my astonishment, it was my mother's hand. She asked in a clear and strong voice, 'Why do you weep so? You are a strong, young man of noble blood with a strong young priestess who loves you and will stand by you through happy times and troubled times. You have everything to be happy for. Why are you so distraught?'"

"I couldn't believe my eyes. It had taken Nila two weeks of constant care and vigil over my mother, and she had cured her. My mother was once again strong. What Nila did with those tears, I never knew. For I did not question her, I was only grateful to her for saving my mother."

Nila's imagination went on further than Blake's story. She just sat there for a moment without response, but letting the events play out in her mind.

Blake said, "Nila, are you okay? What's wrong?"

Nila responded quietly, "I know what she did with the tears. She made an elixir with your tears and her blood and chanted over the elixir. She poured so much of herself into that spell that it almost killed her. That's how she cured your mother. That's why she looked so bad when she opened the door to your mother's chambers. If you recall, it took Nila several weeks to recover from caring for your mother."

Blake was astonished; he didn't know how to respond to this new information. He loved Nila even more for risking her life to save his mother. He was thrilled that her memories were coming forward in Nila's consciousness. "What else do you remember from that life?"

"I'm not sure. I'm not getting clear, concise thoughts—only bits and pieces. I do remember the reason we were forbidden to be together. It was not by your family. It was not because I was a peasant and you were a nobleman. It was forbidden by Lorelei. She threatened to kill all who we loved if we were found together. We were trying to find a way to defeat her when I was captured," Nila told Blake.

"I was captured?" Blake questioned in curiosity. "Don't you mean she was captured?"

"I guess. It's just that it's beginning to get hard to distinguish between her memories from my memories. It really feels that her memories are indeed mine. Something else that's strange is that I feel like I actually went back in time and merged with her and gave her my memories of the future when she was in the cell the night that she died. I feel like I did this to give her strength to face her death and to help her give you strength to wait for her."

Blake replied, "It makes sense because when I first saw her I knew that if she died I could not go on. But then when she reached up and took my hands, her touch calmed me and gave me inner strength. Even though I was frantic at the time knowing that this part of the prophecy would be fulfilled, I knew that I would see her in another life. She wanted me to stay alive and to remember. It was like she knew something that I didn't." Blake took Nila's hand and pressed it against his face.

"I also remember how Lorelei was able to capture Nila and kill her so easily. She cast a binding spell on her. Nila didn't know how to protect herself from this spell. She was powerless. But I know how to cast a protection spell from binding. I remember a Native-American story that my mother used to tell me about a raven that carried the soul of a great shaman out of the reach of evil and to protect it. This is what has to be done. I always thought that it was just an old Cherokee bedtime story. I need to call my mother and ask her exactly how it's done," Nila professed to Blake, very excited that she had a clue about how to protect herself from binding that Lorelei didn't know about.

"That's wonderful!" Blake said excitedly, knowing that this prophecy would end as it should and he would no longer have to be without his soul mate.

"My sweet Blake, can you give me a while to be alone? I need to contact my mother and ask her for guidance in casting the protection spell. I don't want you to leave me or to go very far," Nila begged with her eyes in a way that Blake could never resist.

"Sure. And you know that I would never leave you or be very far from you. I am always there for you," Blake obliged her request. He knew this might be the only way to save his dear Nila.

Chapter 11

Nila waited until Blake had disappeared from sight before she began to call her mother. Even though she no longer saw Blake, she could feel his presence. She knew that he was still very close. She knew that he would be there for her in a split second, if she needed him. This gave her such a comforting feeling.

It was much easier to call upon the spirit of her mother this time, almost effortlessly—like calling out to someone who was only standing two feet away. "Momma, Momma. I really need your help. I need you again. I have remembered something that I think can help me." With those words, a warm and loving arm encircled Nila's waist from behind. She turned with a start to find her mother, Mary Jones, standing behind her.

"I know. You have finally let your shaman spirit guide you. You have remembered the story of the old shaman and the raven," Mary Jones said to her daughter as she circled around to face her. She brushed long, black locks from Nila's eyes, showing the beautiful sparkles of green.

"Oh Momma, you have to teach me how to do this. How do I cast the protection-from-binding spell? This is what I need to do, right?" Nila questioned like a pleading child yearning to learn something new.

Mary Jones smiled at Nila and said, "Yes, my dear. This is how you will defeat Lorelei. You must awaken at dawn on the morning of a new moon. You must take a ritual bath in salt water to cleanse yourself. Go into the woods and recite the poem from the story. The poem is the spell. Once you do that, you will be protected from having your powers bound. When you need it the most, the raven will come and protect your spirit. Do you remember the poem?"

"I do. It was something like this," Nila replied, as she began to recite the poem that she had heard so many times as a child while falling asleep in her mother's arms.

"Come high on the midnight sky,

Mr. Raven to protect my soul,

From anyone who would try,

To take it and forever hold.

Give me the power,

To take from those before,

So that I may tower,

Over my enemies ever more."

Nila's mother just smiled. She was so proud that her daughter had remembered the spell and discovered the way to protect herself. "Yes, Nila, that is the poem. Cast the spell. The raven will do the rest when the time comes. I must go now."

Nila didn't want to see her mother leave again, but she understood that this world was no longer hers and she was lucky to have this time with Mary Jones. With tears in her eyes, she gave her mother a tight hug and bid her farewell in the respect that her mother deserved. "Go now, Momma, in peace and without regret. I release you. I love you and will see you soon. Blessed be."

Mary Jones smiled at her daughter, heart filled with pride for the young woman that she had become. She faded away as she blew Nila an invisible kiss.

Only seconds had passed before Blake emerged from the wooded area. He could sense the loss that Nila felt and knew that her mother had gone. He walked up to her, and she fell into his arms, letting herself become a part of him. He held her tightly, not wanting to ever release her. The wind blew around the entwined bodies of the two young lovers as if it were the spirits of their ancestors giving them their blessing. Nila breathed deeply, taking in the musky scent of Blake, feeling that she could not breathe unless she was breathing in his scent.

Nila's face was buried deep in Blake's chest so when she spoke her words were muffled. "Blake, can we just lie by the lake for awhile? I know what to do now. I know how to cast the protection spell."

Blake pushed her away from him slightly so that he could see her face. "That's great! When can you do it?" he said as he took her hand and guided her to the spot where they had been before. They sat side-by-side with arms around each other, Nila's head leaning against Blake's shoulder and Blake resting his face upon Nila's head.

"It has to be done at dawn on the morning of the next new moon, which is in two days," Nila said, her ear pressed against his chest, hearing the throbbing of his heart.

"What happens then?" Blake asked.

"Then I have to find my inner power to fight Lorelei and trust in the raven to protect my soul."

Blake gently nudged Nila with his hand, guiding her to lie back. She didn't resist him. Nila gladly obliged Blake. She just wanted to lay in Blake's arms and rest. She wanted to forget the world and only be aware of Blake. Neither spoke. Nila fell asleep almost immediately. The dreams flooded her mind like raging waters.

Nila found herself with Blake at the base of a tall tree with towering limbs reaching out over them. Blake was carving their names into the tree. Nila recognized the tree; she had seen it before. This was the tree where Blake had killed the soldier; it was also the tree outside the art room window. It was Nila's muse! Nila understood the importance of the tree. When Blake spilled the blood of the soldier to save Nila, he gave a blood oath of undying eternal love to her. This is where she must confront Lorelei; this is where Nila would be the strongest.

Then Nila saw her mother. Two women were with her mother. They approached, and Nila questioned, "Momma, who are these women?"

"They are your ancestors. They are the sisters. We have come to explain how you will gain your full powers. Nila, you don't come into full power, your birthright, until the day you become 17½. Lorelei knows this. She killed the first Nila the night before she turned 17½," Nila's mother explained.

Nila quickly interrupted, "But I turn 17½ in six days. Will I be ready?"

"Lorelei bound the first Nila's power before she could accept her birthright and kept her from coming into full power. She knows that she is no match for you once you have your birthright, so she will try to do the same as before. The difference now is that you can protect yourself from the binding and she will never be the wiser. To gain your birthright, all you have to do is be open and accept it when it comes to you," Mary Jones explained.

"How will I know when it comes to me?"

"You will know. There will be no mistaking it. It will feel like electricity is flowing through you. You will instantly know things and see things in a different way. All of your senses will be awakened. You will feel the power within you. You will just know. And we will be there. When you feel the need for us, just call upon us. Blessed be." With those words, Mary and the sisters were gone. Nila stood there alone in her dream not sure of what to do next. Suddenly, things changed.

Nila felt as if she were flying. She saw a devastated Blake and the wizard who had helped him. Her heart sank, she couldn't stand to see Blake in such a state. She wept so hard that she awoke

Nila sat up quickly. Blake sprang to her side, held her tightly, and asked what was wrong. Nila answered, "I had a dream of us carving our names into the tree at school. Then I saw my mother and the sisters. They told me about coming into my birthright. Then I saw you broken and devastated, talking with the wizard. I cried so hard, because you were terribly saddened by the loss of Nila, that I woke myself up."

"Did you hear what the wizard told me?" Blake asked.

"No. I couldn't stand to see you like that. I didn't want to bear witness to any of it," Nila replied.

"You need to know. The wizard told me many things and did things to help us. After saving me, not only did he make me immortal, he also cast an invisibility spell on me so that Lorelei wouldn't know that I was alive all of these years. When the spell was cast, Lorelei could no longer sense me and thought I had died."

"Lorelei has waited all theses years to get what she lost so long ago, me, her prize. She knows of the prophecy—that we will be reborn together. What she is unaware of is that I didn't die, and I remember everything and now you remember everything. We are prepared this time, not like before. She is the one who is unprepared. And with her abundant false confidence, she has no chance," Blake explained to Nila.

"The wizard also told me that because I had killed the soldier to save you that the spilled blood created a blood oath—an eternal bond between you and I. Because the blood was spilled in violence due to Lorelei, this is where we must lure Lorelei," Blake continued.

"I know, I discovered that in my dream," Nila told Blake.

"But the blood oath is not the only reason to fight her at the tree. The soul of the soldier has been trapped there all these years. The only way for it to be released is by him helping the one he once offended—you, Nila. The soldier will help you defeat Lorelei. You have many allies this time—something that she doesn't have," Blake concluded as he reached up and cupped Nila's face in his hand. Her skin felt like the soft, downy feathers of an angel's wing. In fact, he thought that she looked like an angel dropped straight from heaven into his arms and that God meant for him to protect her. That is exactly what Blake intended to do.

Nila responded by nuzzling her face against his hand and closing her eyes, enjoying the reassuring feel of his touch and the scent of his skin. She felt that God had sent Blake to her to protect her. She knew that he would give his life for her.

Nila felt a surge of confidence and waves of pleasure from being so close to Blake. Nila was at ease now, knowing she could exact her pound of flesh from Lorelei for all the evil and pain Lorelei had inflicted on her and others. Nila felt the warmth of Blake's breath on her face as he leaned in to whisper into her ear.

"Nila, know this. These lips that have touched yours will never speak an untrue word to you. You know this by the pleasure that they bring. And my will and my body shall never deny you any wish that I am capable of granting." With those words, Blake's lips lightly grazed Nila's cheek with such a gentleness that Nila was scarcely sure that he had actually kissed her.

Nila needed the closeness of being with Blake. He was the source of her confidence and strength. She turned her face so that her lips met his. It felt right. He parted her lips with his tongue and found refuge inside. He loved her more than he could tell her with words. But she knew the extent of his endless love expressed through his touch, his kisses, and the way he looked at her. Nila obligingly opened her mouth to receive his kiss. She poured her emotions into that kiss. Blake felt himself losing control. He felt her body tremble beneath his hands and knew that she had already lost control. He knew that he had to be strong. But he couldn't.

He had waited so many years to be with her once again, to hold her, to gaze upon her, to love her. The day had grown into dusk, and they were alone. Blake felt as though it were 1728 again. He let his emotions run free and his hands explore the length of Nila's body. She moved with him.

Nila invited Blake's advances. She was not only feeling her own emotions but those of the first Nila. She knew that this was right and good. She knew that this was meant to be. Nila felt the hardness of Blake pressing against her thigh as he hovered over her, propping himself up slightly on his elbow with his hand cupped under Nila's head. His other hand was caressing Nila's body, bringing her to the brink.

Blake's kisses became harder with the growing ecstasy. Nila felt the hot sting of his tongue as he grazed the flesh of her neck and breasts. She pulled him tightly, feeling as though she could not get close enough. Nila entwined her fingers in his dark waves, pressing against the back of his head, forcing his kisses to be stronger. She let her fingers glide under his shirt and explore his lean physique and then further down to the essence of his manhood. Blake quaked beneath her soft, delicate fingers.

Blake crumbled at her desire—at his desire. He slid his hand up under her skirt and gently removed the one and only obstacle of their union. He freed himself and positioned his body into place. Nila stared intently into his eyes as he readied himself. "Nila, are you sure this is what you want?" Blake asked, ready to abort any time if she changed her mind.

"I am. This is destiny. I am not whole without you," Nila pleaded, fearing that Blake would stop.

He did not. Nila's body exploded into euphoria upon Blake's entrance. Everything changed. Everything was now right with the world and with Blake. Nila smiled as Blake looked down upon her beauty writhing with desire and wanton in his eyes. Nila didn't want this moment to ever end. She wanted their union to be permanent, to have him inside of her forever. She pulled him in closer, feeling like she could never have him close enough to her. As Nila's fingers slid up and down Blake's back, she could feel him tremble beneath her touched. She was pleased to know that she had this effect upon him. She was sure that he knew that he had the same effect upon her. With one last burst of euphoria, Nila knew that this encounter had come an end.

Upon the consummation of their love, Blake raised his head up from her neck and looked in Nila's eyes. She knew what she saw in his eyes was a love that no other had or will ever experience in the existence of humankind. Tears of joy streamed down Nila's face. Blake collapsed upon Nila as they held each other tightly. The only words that were spoken, that needed to be spoken, were "I love you." They lay in each other's arms—content and fulfilled.

Nila heard a whisper in her ear. It was the whisper of a woman. It was her mother's voice. "Your union with Blake will make you stronger." Nila smiled at the approval of her mother. However, Nila knew that her grandmother was probably worrying. "Blake, I should probably go home now. I know that Grandma is beginning to worry." As she looked into his eyes, knowing that there was no way they could ever be apart again, she asked, "But will you please stay with me tonight?"

"Yes. But won't your grandmother and father mind?"

"I really don't think so. I'm pretty sure that my mother has already prepared them for us."

"I don't ever want to be without you again. There is no other place I would rather be than in your arms."

They gathered their things and headed back to Nila's house.

Chapter 12

The next morning, Nila awoke with great confidence at having Blake lying by her side, staring at her. "Did you sleep at all last night?" she asked her nobleman.

"Not much. I had been so long without you, I just wanted to look at you and take in the beauty that I had been without so many years. What do we do today?"

"I guess we go to school like two normal teenagers for the next few days, and then I'll learn all that I can from my grandmother in the evenings until the day comes to face Lorelei," Nila said as she absentmindedly stroked Lilly's head who was laying curled up beside her.

"And do you want me to go back home?"

"No way. I'm not letting you go anywhere," Nila said, as she leaned up and gave him a quick kiss on the mouth. "I need you with me."

Blake grabbed her and held her in his arms as if they were freshly reunited. "Then it is by your side I shall remain, my beautiful peasant priestess."

"But do you think that it will be alright with your aunt?" Nila questioned, all the while fearing the answer would be no.

"Well, I have a confession to make. I don't really have an aunt, obviously. All of my relatives have long since died, including my aunts."

"I thought that maybe the wizard may have given you a guardian or something."

"No, it's always just been me. No one to answer to. So your wish is my command, my darling peasant priestess," Blake responded seductively. Blake's smile made Nila's will go weak with desire.

"Well, I guess we should get ready and go on to school as usual. I know Sherry is going to have questions as to what's going on," Nila said as she reached over to check her phone for messages. She held her phone out to Blake, "See, there's like 20 texts from Sherry."

Blake pushed Nila's hair from her face and pulled her in for a long and deep kiss, "As you wish." He pushed the covers back and retreated to the bathroom.

Nila lay there a few minutes reveling in the wonder of what she had recently discovered—a love that was almost three centuries old. As she heard the water running, her imagination went back to when she had seen Blake's nakedness at the lake just a few days earlier. She crept to the bathroom and stood slightly behind the partially opened door, peaking around the other side, trying to get a glimpse of Blake in the shower. Nila knew that all she had to do was say the word and Blake would strip down before her. But she didn't want to seem too naive or even too forward.

Nila knew that it didn't matter that she was secretly watching Blake in the shower when she heard, "Do you want to join me?" Blake's sensual voice came from behind the curtain. She didn't want to ask how he knew that she was there. She was sure that it was the same way that he always knew when she was in need.

Unsure of how she really felt about him seeing her totally nude and unsure of what her reaction should be, Nila fell over her words, "Um, sure, if you don't mind."

"I would love it," Blake pulled back the shower curtain that clung to the oval ring that hung from the ceiling over the tub.

Nila was surprised at how easy it was to drop her clothes to the floor before Blake. Blake was in awe at her beautiful bare body. He pulled the shower curtain back for Nila to enter the tub. He held out his hand to her. She slipped her hand into his as he helped her into the warm water that was raining on the porcelain.

When Nila looked into Blake's eyes, it was an automatic response to fall into his strong, protective arms. He felt so warm and so hard. She felt so soft and delicate. With the water streaming down their faces, Nila stood slightly on her toes and reached up to kiss Blake. The kiss was so sensual because of the warm water and friction of their exposed skin. All they could think of was how much they wanted each other. Blake's hands sought out every part of Nila's body—perfection and imperfection alike. His lips had no boundaries; they explored Nila from head to toe. Nila did not protest in any way. She was breathless. Her chest heaved up and down like she had just run a marathon. Blake gently guided her down to her knees and turned her away from him. He positioned himself behind her. Nila welcomed him. He knew this by the way she arched her back and threw her head back. The water added to the affect as it glided gently across their bodies. It wasn't long before they both reached the climax of their love.

Exhausted, Nila rolled over and lay back in the tub, letting the water run across her body and into her face. Blake towered over her. She was amazed at how pleasing he was to look at. She just wanted to pull him down on her and start all over, but she knew that there would be plenty of time for that after Lorelei was no longer a threat.

Blake washed her with such ease and gentleness. He then washed himself as the water continued to bead on her body. He rinsed himself and then her. Blake turned the faucet handles to off and helped Nila back out onto the bathmat. He took a towel and dried her thoroughly, drinking in the sight of her beauty with his eyes. He then dried himself. They both dressed, neither saying a word. No words needed to be said.

They met Ruth Jones for breakfast. Nila's grandmother smiled at the young couple as she greeted them, "Did you sleep well?"

Nila shook her head in response, and Blake answered, "Yes, ma'am."

"Well, I trust you two are hungry," Ruth Jones said with a devious smile on her face.

Nila blushed knowing that her grandmother was not a naive woman, "Yes, Grandma, we are a bit hungry. Is Daddy still home?"

"No. He is already gone. Don't worry about him. He knows what I know, and he is okay with it. Your father and mother were about your age, too."

"Grandma!" Nila squeaked between bites of bacon as Blake spit orange juice out into his napkin.

Ruth Jones just laughed.

"How did you know?"

"For one, this is almost 300 years in the making. Two, your mother made a little spiritual visit to your father and I last night. Three, you both have that look about you. Now eat up, I'm sure you need it," Ruth said as she giggled and took her plate to the table.

Nila and Blake quickly ate their breakfast, told Ruth goodbye, and left for school. They were at Legacy High before they knew it. Blake walked around his car and opened the car door for Nila. Nila felt like the entire school was watching when Blake reached out for her hand. She obligingly took it as he helped her out. They walked into the school, arms wrapped around one another.

Sherry and Kevin were standing by the front doors all cuddled up together. "Well, well, well, Nila. What have you two been up to?"

"Sherry," Nila pleaded silently with her not to go there.

"Come on, Nile's. I'm just joking," Sherry sighed. She pulled Nila to the side, leaving the guys to talk. "Seriously, though, I can tell. How did it happen? I want all the details."

"How can you tell?"

"You have a look of relief and satisfaction on your faces. And you are looking at each other like you could eat each other up," Sherry giggled.

"Okay, you're right. We went there. But there is so much more that I need to tell you, but not now. At lunch, I'll tell you and Kevin everything."

"What is it?"

"I will tell you at lunch," Nila said, as she turned and walked to Blake.

"Okay, I'll see you at lunch," Sherry called out as Nila walked into the school with Blake.

Blake walked Nila to each class. Before long, they found themselves in art class. There was trouble sitting at their table.

"Well, good morning Nila, Blake," Dawn said in a sarcastic voice. "Where were you two yesterday?"

"Not that it's any of your business, but we spent the day together," Nila started.

Blake interjected, "And a wonderful day at that." Blake leaned in and kissed Nila lightly on the lips.

Dawn jumped up with pure evil in her eyes. Her chair crashed against the floor, bringing everyone's attention to the three.

"Dawn, is there a problem?" Mrs. Carver thundered, making everyone snap their heads in her direction in total surprise and utter disbelief.

Dawn didn't say a word. She stormed past Mrs. Carver and out the door. No one could believe what was happening. Mrs. Carver had never lost her temper, and Dawn had never been so defiant, even though she was spoiled. Nila was especially surprised.

"Alright class, we've got work to do. Get started on your projects." Mrs. Carver went to her desk and quietly sat.

Nila and Blake sat at their table. Nila couldn't help but stare at the old tree. "I see that tree, the tree that I have looked at the entire time I have been at this school, and had no idea why it pulled me so. Now that I know, it feels so strange but very reassuring." Nila looked in the direction of the plump, sweet art teacher. "The entire time I have known Mrs. Carver, I have never seen her like that. Even though it was quite startling, it was at the same time reassuring."

Blake was unsure of how he should respond. "Do you have any idea what just happened?"

"Not at all, but it was like a storm and the extreme calm afterwards."

It didn't take long for the mood in art class to lighten up and go back to normal. Nila and Blake sat with Sherry and Kevin in lunch. Nila caught Sherry up on everything that happened since they last spoke. Sherry couldn't believe what she was hearing. "This is all interesting, but I want to hear about other things, you know."

Nila's face flushed, "Later on that subject, please."

"Well, let's go to the little girl's room, shall we?" Sherry prodded.

Nila agreed, knowing that Sherry was not going to drop this. "Sure." The two best friends went to the closest bathroom. As soon as they were through the doors, Sherry began. "Tell me everything, don't leave out any details."

Nila told Sherry about her and Blake. She didn't leave out any details. Nila was surprised at how it lifted her spirits to share this with her friend. Sherry squealed, "I knew it. I told you that first day something was up with your dream man. I knew you two would end up together. Just be very careful with all this Lorelei and reincarnation stuff. If you need me for anything, let me know. And watch Dawn. She's been acting strange the past couple of days."

"I know. She was messing with me and Blake in art and was extremely rude to Mrs. Carver. What was even stranger was Mrs. Carver's reaction. She thundered out at Dawn. She really lost her temper."

"That's weird."

"Yeah, I know.

Chapter 13

The days passed. Sherry gave Nila space. Nila and Blake had grown even closer. Dawn had not returned to school. Ruth Jones had been teaching Nila all she could think of that might help her. It was the night of the full moon, the night of the protection-from-binding ritual. It was nearing midnight, and Nila was preparing her ritual bath.

"Hey, do you need me to do anything?" Blake opened the bathroom door slightly. He was trying to engage Nila in conversation. She had been withdrawn and in a world of her own that day, not really letting anyone in.

"No, I'm good. Thanks, though," replied Nila while sitting on the side of the tub, adjusting water temperature. Nila didn't turn around to face Blake as she spoke. She was choking back tears that she did not want him to see. She did not want him know that she was having a moment of weakness. The last thing Nila wanted was for him to worry any more about her.

Blake was at the end of his rope. He couldn't stand feeling shut out by Nila. Slowly, Blake pushed through the partially opened door and came up behind her, kneeling down, and wrapping his arms around her. He buried his face in her neck, taking in the scent that no other had.

As strong as Nila wanted to be, she just let it all go when she felt his safe, strong arms around her. She knew that she must confide her feelings to Blake. He could handle it; he was her protector. Nila turned in his arms, tears streaming down her face. She reached up and held him tightly in her arms.

Blake pulled back, "Hey, what's this all about?" He gently brushed her hair back from her tear-soaked face, held her face between his hands, and kissed her forehead. "Nila, tell me."

"I just don't think I can do this."

"It's a simple ritual."

"I know, but when I do this, it means this thing with Lorelei is real."

"Oh, my beautiful peasant priestess, its real whether you perform the ritual or not. This is for your protection.

This is one more step in making you stronger than you already are."

Nila leaned in and held him as tightly as she possibly could. "I know. I just feel so unsure."

"That's a good thing. It means you're not overconfident. Overconfidence is always the undoing of great people." Blake tried to give a reassuring smile. But the truth of the matter was that Blake was also feeling uncertain about their fate.

Behind all the tears, Nila smiled back knowing that Blake would be there to protect her. After this ritual, not only would she be protected from binding but it would allow her to gain her birthright and have her ancestors stand by her, making her invincible. "You're right. I can do this but I need you, the raven, and my ancestors to stand by my side."

"And that means?"

"That means first I need to perform this ritual before it's too late."

"Right. Now take that bath. It's almost midnight." Blake hugged Nila in those safe arms for a brief moment and kissed her so passionately that she felt her knees grow weak. With that, Blake left her side, and closed the bathroom door behind him. He lay back on the bed with

Lilly and waited on Nila. He couldn't be with her during the ritual, but he did have to be alert in case she needed him.

Nila finished her ritual bath. Still wet, she put on her robe. She opened the door. "Blake I'm ready. Are you going with me to the woods?"

"Of course." Blake stood, leaving Lilly sleeping soundly on the bed. He took Nila's hand, and they descended the stairs to find her grandmother and father waiting on the couch.

"Are you ready, Nila girl?" Ruth asked as she stood to greet Nila.

"I am, Grandma." Nila leaned over and embraced her grandmother.

Nila's father stood and hugged his daughter like she was a tiny girl leaving for her first overnight trip away from home. "Nila, you are so much stronger than any of us. But you must still use caution. I am so very proud of the young woman that you have become. I love you,"

"I love you, Daddy," Nila said, giving her father a lingering hug. "Okay, it's almost 12:00. I will be back in a few minutes." Nila took Blake's hand, and he walked her into the woods behind the old farmhouse.

Blake slipped Nila's robe off her nude body and draped it across a nearby tree limb. He then knelt on one knee in front of Nila's exposed body and took her hand in his. "My peasant priestess, I vow an eternal oath of protection and love to you. I vow to give my life to protect you. I will always hold you in my heart." Blake kissed her hand and bowed his head.

Nila tugged at his hand to silently suggest standing. He obeyed her silent demand and stood before her beauty. "Blake, I know that you are my protector. I know that you would give your life for me. But I could not be as strong as you have been. I could not live without you. I would give my life for you."

"Nila, I know that. You have already done that once—in 1728. You weren't just caught. You gave yourself up to Lorelei. She sent hunters out to kill me. She said that if she could not have me, then I should die. You went to her and bargained for my life. You gave yours so that I could live," Blake wept.

"It will not be that way this time. It does not have to be that way this time." As Nila kissed him, they breathed life into each other.

"It's time now, go to the edge of the woods. If anything happens, just call me."

"I will. I love you."

"I love you," Blake reluctantly walked away, leaving Nila alone and exposed in the woods that were lit only by the moonlight.

Nila heard rustling in the leaves just a few feet away from her in the trees. She was not fearful, she knew that it was the raven. So she called out to him. "Raven, I beg to you, come to me." Nila held her arms outstretched, reaching to the sky.

"Come high on the midnight sky,

Mr. Raven to protect my soul,

From anyone who would try,

For take it and forever hold.

Give me the power,

To take from those before,

So that I may tower,

Over my enemies ever more."

The raven appeared from the trees, squawking at Nila. It sounded like bird sounds. However, Nila understood everything that the bird was trying to relate to her.

"Nila Anna Jones, you call upon me to protect your soul. You are indeed worthy of my protection, and I will grant it. However, you must accept the consequences," the bird said.

"What are your consequences, Mr. Raven? I will accept anything you require of me other than harm to my loved ones."

The bird laughed heartily, "Oh, you naïve girl. I am a protector of souls. Why would I harm anyone with an honest and righteous heart? The thing you must accept is physical pain. You must let me enter your soul."

"I accept your terms."

"Then you should drop to your knees because this will cause much agony."

Nila did as the great bird commanded. She readied herself for the unexpected. The raven took the form of a dark cloud and forced its way into Nila's body. She cried out in pain. Nila had never known such pain—even in death as the first Nila. She lay writhing on the ground as the bird became one with her.

Blake emerged from the trees. He tried to run to her but was hit with an invisible barrier. He desperately cried out, knowing that he had failed her again. "Nila! Nila! Please leave her alone! This can't happen! You can't take her from me. I just found her again!"

Nila fell still. Blake knew that she must be dead. The barrier fell, and Blake ran to her side. He sat beside her and scooped her limp, cold body into his arms. He cried out in despair and wept. Nila stirred slightly. Her face was wet with tears, her hair and body were soaked with sweat, and she was breathing shallowly.

"Nila, Nila. Are you okay? Come on, Nila, you can't leave me again. This was supposed to be a ritual of protection," Blake cuddled her and kissed her on her unresponsive lips.

Nila slowly opened her eyes, weakly reached up, and gave Blake a weak hug. He pulled her in tightly and closely. "Nila, are you alright?"

"I'm just really weak, that's all."

"Did something go wrong? Why was it so painful?"

"Nothing went wrong. Everything is as it should be. The raven is now a part of me. It was very painful—his entrance and convergence with my soul. It is a consequence for accepting his protection. It cannot be painless. But I am okay. It worked. But I really need to rest now."

Blake grabbed Nila's robe and wrapped her in it. He carefully picked her up and carried her back to the farmhouse. Fearful of her health, Blake gently laid her on the couch. He methodically explained everything that he knew about what had happened in the woods to Ruth and David. Ruth, of course, knew what was wrong with Nila. She knew that it had been very painful and tiring to accept the raven. Ruth retrieved a cool, damp washcloth from the kitchen and sponged Nila. David sat beside her and held her hand. He pushed her wet black hair from her face.

Nila knew that she was both weak and strong. She felt that it took everything she had to offer in accepting the raven as part of her. She also knew that she was now stronger because of the raven's protection. She closed her eyes and slept.

Chapter 14

Nila awoke in Blake's strong arms. She felt different than she had ever felt before in her life. She felt strong. Everything was going to be alright. However, the face-off with Lorelei would not be an easy one. What price would have to be paid in order to win that battle?

Blake was sleeping soundly. Nila tried to slip out of his arms. That did not work. Blake woke immediately. "Where do you think you're going without me?" he smiled lazily.

"I thought I might start getting ready for school."

"You mean steal all of the hot water?" Blake joked.

"Sure, that's it," Nila playfully smacked Blake on the arm. "Actually, do you want to join me or go first?"

"No thanks, I think I'm going to lay here with Lilly a few more minutes. Go ahead. Take your time," Blake lay there with Lilly snuggled up against him. He closed his eyes contently. It was a look that made Nila feel happy and satisfied. He was more at ease because she had the added protection of the raven.

"I love you, Blake, my sweet nobleman." Nila leaned over and lightly brushed her delicate, soft lips against Blake's neck. As her lips touched his skin, she breathed in, deeply tasting the scent of him with her nose. Simultaneously, without opening his eyes, Blake whispered in her ear, "I love you, Nila, my peasant priestess."

Nila walked onto the cold bathroom floor. She could feel every imperfection under her feet. She adjusted the water and stepped into the tub. Each bead of water caressed her flesh. She savored every moment of that shower. Her senses were heightened. Nila could hear every single bird individually that was chirping outside her window. She could hear the rise and fall of Blake's breathing.

After showering, Nila slipped out of the bedroom, careful not to wake Blake. She crept down the steps to the kitchen, knowing that her grandmother would be making breakfast. She found Ruth Jones standing in front of the kitchen stove. "Good morning, Grandma."

Ruth turned to greet her granddaughter and was surprised to see she had a gold glow. "Nila, how do you feel? You look different. You look almost like you're glowing gold. You look confident and rested."

"I feel really good. But I can hear extra well, feel and smell very well. It seems like my senses are super-sensitive. What's going on?"

"The union with the raven was successful. You are fine. It's all natural. You now have his heightened senses." Ruth leaned over and hugged her granddaughter. "Here, have some breakfast." She put her hand in the small of Nila's back and guided her to the table.

"Thanks, Grandma," Nila said as she retrieved a cat-head biscuit from a bowl on the table and placed it on her plate. She heard Blake upstairs stirring. "Sounds like Blake's up."

"I don't hear anything. Are you sure?"

"Don't you hear him?"

"It's that raven."

Then Blake came into the kitchen. "Good morning." Blake leaned in and kissed Nila on the neck. "Good morning, Mrs. Jones."

"Good morning, Blake. Fix you a plate. Eat up," Ruth said, as she handed Blake a plate.

The three ate. Nila and Blake finished getting ready and hurried off for school. The two young lovers pulled into Legacy High. Just as Blake put the car in park, Nila lost all sense of time. She felt totally displaced from everything familiar. She found herself alone in a white mist.

"I'm back. You did not survive my wrath before and you will not survive it this time, and the boy will be mine," a disembodied voice came from the mist.

Nila was fearful, but she remembered the raven was with her. She tried to calm and steady herself. A voice from within said, "My darling, the raven will protect you. Give in to him, and let him fly you back to Blake." Nila gave all her will to the raven, "Mr. Raven, protect me. Take me back to Blake. Take me from this evil." She was roused by Blake shaking her by the shoulders.

"Nila, are you okay?"

"Blake, she's here. She has found me," Nila replied breathlessly.

"Lorelei?"

"Yes. She pulled me from here out into a white mist. She said that she was back for me. I didn't respond. My mother's voice came to me and told me to call upon the raven. I did, and I came back here to you."

Blake held Nila securely, letting her know that she was safe. "So, she has found you. Does she know I'm here?"

"I don't think so. She didn't call you by name. She said that the boy would be hers."

"We now know that you do have the protection of the raven, your mother is there to help, and she hasn't found me. This is good. We have so many things going for us that she is unaware of," Blake sighed in a relief.

The next few days were intense for Nila with Lorelei randomly pulling Nila out of her reality. Lorelei tormented Nila. Nila was brave and did not give up anything to the evil witch. At first, the voice of Lorelei was totally foreign. But then it became familiar to her. Recognizable. She knew that voice but could not place it.

Nila made it through those unsettling days okay. But one night, after she and Blake had fallen into a deep sleep, Nila's heightened senses kicked in. She felt as if someone was standing over her, watching her and Blake sleep. Her eyes opened to see someone hovering over her just inches from her face. She wanted to scream. She tried to scream. But she couldn't. Nila tried to move, but she was paralyzed. Nila tried to telepathically rouse Blake from his slumber but to no avail.

Lorelei was going to murder her then and there. The witch gritted through her teeth, "I'm coming back for you. I want to play with you, first. Make you wish for death. Welcome it when the time comes." Nila gazed upon Blake's motionless, unaware body, "And he will be mine this time."

Fear rippled down Nila's spine, causing her to shiver. The witch's hair whipped at her face. Lorelei's hands clinched her throat. Nila knew that she was going die. She was losing consciousness. She felt weak. The room closed in on her. All Nila could see was the face of the woman who had killed her almost 300 years ago. The witch glared into Nila's eyes. Lorelei was penetrating her very soul. When Nila felt her life slipping away, Lorelei disappeared.

Nila bolted upright in her bed, gasping for air. Blake awoke to find Nila pale and struggling to breathe. Her skin was as cold as fresh spring water. "Nila, Nila. What is it? What happened?"

Gasping, Nila responded, "It was Lorelei. She was here. I tried to move, to scream, to wake you, but I couldn't. She was inches from my face. She said that she was going to play with me and make me welcome death when it came. She saw you. She looked directly at you. She said that she would have you this time. She was strangling me, and then just disappeared." Nila whispered in a small voice, barely audible, "I thought that I was going to die."

Blake wrapped her in his arms, "Nila, its okay. She can't hurt you. Your mother is with you, the raven is with you. She's trying to weaken you with fear."

Nila pulled back, "But why couldn't I gain control over my body?"

"Did you call upon your mother or the raven?"

"No."

"Why?"

"I'm not sure. I guess I let the fear take control."

"Okay. That's good. You realize what you should have done. It was your first real confrontation with her in this life. Now you know what to expect. You know what to do next time. Control your fear and call upon the raven, call upon your mother, and call to me. Your fear is what blocked your cries from me. Control your fear."

As the days passed, Lorelei's presence became more intense. Nila felt like she might lose her mind. When she felt like she could take no more, she called upon the raven for protection like her mother had told her. This went on until the day came, that fateful day, the day before Nila was accept her birthright and come into full power.

Chapter 15

Nila was restless all night. She found it extremely difficult to sleep. Blake was also uneasy. Nila's restlessness kept him from sleeping well. That day and night would be trying for them both and very dangerous for all involved.

Nila rolled into Blake's arms to face him. "Did you sleep?"

"Not really. We are both facing something massive tonight, and getting through the day is not going to be easy at all." Blake filled his arms with the soft, beautiful flesh of his peasant priestess. Trying to sound confident and brave, all the while being frightened and unsure, "Remember to control your fear. It will be okay. Lorelei has no idea that the raven is protecting you. You are so strong. And once you have come into your full power, she will be no match for you."

Nila was lost in Blake's magnificent blue eyes. She felt safe and secure when she looked into his eyes. Today, she did not only feel good but powerful, maybe even invincible. "I will control my fear. I remember how the first Nila felt as she was dying. She wasn't fearful of dying, only of losing you. It was the most painful feeling I have ever experienced. I will not go through that again. I know that I can do this. It's hard to believe that only a few weeks ago I had no boyfriend, thought I would be a virgin for all eternity, and just a plain girl—nothing special. Today, I have you, am about to become a very powerful being, and have this enormous responsibility. So many things have happened. I know they have happened for a reason, and it can't be to fail." Nila snuggled in closer to Blake and took a deep breath, loving that scent that she had come to know so well.

"Well, school or no school?" Blake smiled down at Nila and then gave her a light kiss on the lips.

Nila thought for a minute as she bit on her lower lip. "Um, how about a half a day?"

"Which half?"

"Let's go to the first half, then leave at lunch and relax by the lake for a while since we have so many fond memories that were made there. Maybe we can add to them?"

Nila's smile and suggestion tied Blake's heart in a knot. He could not deny her the request.

"That sounds wonderful." Blake smacked her playfully on the ass. "What are we waiting for? Let's make some memories."

The young lovers got ready, ate a quick breakfast, and went off to school. Nila felt kind of bad because she was in such a hurry and barely said two words to her grandmother. Little did she know that Ruth Jones wasn't in a talking mood anyway. She was concerned about what her granddaughter was to face that night.

They were at Legacy High in a blink of an eye. "We're here," Blake said. He leaned over, kissed Nila, and let his hand find a place on the top of her right hip.

Nila couldn't decide whether it was the soft, sensual touch of his lips that were making her have that wanton feeling or if it was the feel of his warm hand on her hip, knowing that his hand was likely to explore other parts of her body. Nila responded breathlessly, "Okay, we should probably stop this or we won't be going in at all."

"Agreed," Blake smiled sweetly. He stepped out of the car and walked over to let Nila out. They walked into school hand-in-hand and so in love.

They saw Sherry and Kevin standing by Sherry's locker. "Hey guys. I didn't think you would be here today. You know, the big day and all," Sherry said.

"We wanted to have some normalcy and try to forget about the big day until the time comes so we came on to school like two normal teens." Nila felt a knot in the pit of stomach.

Sherry realized the discomfort she had caused Nila by mentioning the day. She so regretted that. She had always been there for Nila, trying to protect her. "I'm sorry Nila, I didn't mean to upset you."

Nila tried to give the façade that she was okay. "You didn't. I'm fine. Really. I'm just looking forward to having this all over with." Blake stepped a little closer to Nila and smiled. The warmth of his closeness comforted her.

"Well, we should really get to class. I can't afford another tardy. One more, and it's after school for me." Kevin tugged at Sherry and motioned his head toward his first class, trying to dispel the uncomfortable feeling that clung in the air around them.

"Yeah, we should go. But seriously, Niles, if you need anything tonight, call me. Or if you want, I can be with you to help." Sherry's protectiveness came forward.

"Niles, I will be there too if you need me. My grandma always says that I have a hidden strength. And one day it will help me to achieve something very important." Kevin stepped in slightly toward Nila and took her hand in his.

Nila felt oddly comforted by his touch. A warm wave of security swept across her like she only experienced when Blake touched her. She was unsure of how to process this. "Thank you, guys, but it is going to be extremely dangerous. I really don't want you to get hurt. I love you two so much, and thank you for wanting to help. It will be okay, I promise." Kevin let go of her hand, but Nila felt surprised by the longing for his touch.

"Okay, but if you change your mind, let us know," Kevin said.

Sherry and Kevin joined hands and turned to walk away. "Oh, Nila, I hate to drop this bombshell on you, but the bitch is back. You know, Dawn Gale."

"That's okay. We're only staying for half a day. What was wrong with her, anyway?" Nila asked with one eyebrow cocked up.

"Don't know. Don't care," Sherry shrugged. She and Kevin headed down the hall. "Remember, Niles, we're only a text away. Be careful," Sherry said over her shoulder.

"Thanks, guys."

Before Nila knew it, she and Blake were in art. And so was Dawn. "Crap," Nila mumbled under her breath.

Blake moved closer to Nila and slightly in front of her in a protective stance. "Its okay. We're leaving after this class. Mrs. Carver won't let her mess with you."

"I know. She just looks crazy, though. She's a mess." Nila couldn't believe her eyes. It appeared that Dawn hadn't brushed her teeth. She looked like she probably hadn't bathed or changed clothes in a couple of days. Her nails were chipped, her hair was unkempt, and she had no makeup on. Dawn looked so tired. Even Mrs. Carver did a double-take when she walked into the room.

Chills ran down Nila's spine as Dawn looked into Nila's eyes. Dawn's eyes looked wild, hollow, and empty. Nila knew that the eyes were the windows to the soul, and it appeared to Nila that Dawn was actually soulless.

As Dawn gave Nila a stare that would frighten the Devil himself, she gritted through her teeth, growling like a rabid animal, "WHAT?"

Nila was caught off guard. "Um, are you okay?"

"Just peachy."

"Okay then." Nila and Blake walked on to their seats at Nila's table. She sat so that she could see her muse. She knew that she would soon be back there at the school, actually at that tree to face down that evil bitch, Lorelei.

Nila was surprised to see that only about 10 minutes into class Dawn laid her head on the table and went to sleep. Mrs. Carver did not bother to wake her. Nila thought that Mrs. Carver was happy just to have Dawn's mouth shut during class, so she left well enough alone. Art class was otherwise uneventful. The bell rang before they knew it. Dawn woke up and meandered out of the class without so much as a word to anyone.

Nila couldn't wait to get out of school and somewhere alone with Blake so that she could try to get her mind off of what she was about to face that night. But she had to see if Mrs. Carver knew what was going on with Dawn. Nila had never liked Dawn, but she couldn't help but be concerned over another soul who appeared in need of help. "Mrs. Carver," Nila said quietly, as she approached the smiling art teacher.

"Yes, Nila." Mrs. Carver looked up with that tender smile that made Nila know that all was right with the world, even if it really wasn't. Mrs. Carver had a way about her that made everyone feel better.

"What's wrong with Dawn? I know she's not my favorite person in the world. But she really looks very pitiful, sad, and lonely."

"I wouldn't worry too much about Dawn. I don't really know what's going on with her, but I think it may be a touch of karma coming around to bite her in the butt. Seriously, she's a resilient girl. She'll be just fine. Really. You just worry about what's important to you. Keep your mind focused on Nila. You appear to have a lot on your mind these days. I'll keep an eye on Dawn. Promise." Mrs. Carver laid her hand on Nila's shoulder. Nila felt warmth from head to toe like an angel had touched her—a reassuring feeling.

Only a second later, Nila had an odd flash of her past life. She saw the chambermaid who had helped Blake escape. Nila was sure that it was her friend, the chambermaid. Nila recognized her old friend. It was odd. She had never seen her before in this life, but she knew exactly who it was when she saw her. She had no idea why she had a vision of her old friend. It was so strange, but Nila brushed it off in a hurry to leave the school and Dawn behind her.

Blake lightly took Nila by the elbow with his hand and tugged her gently. "Are you ready, Nila?"

Nila responded with a slight nod of her head, letting small black wisps of hair fall forward and graze her neck. It caught Blake's attention, making his body ache for her. "Yeah, sure." Then she looked at Mrs. Carver. "I'll see you tomorrow."

"Goodbye, Nila." Mrs. Carver immediately directed her attention elsewhere.

Nila turned to walk out of the art room with Blake. His hand dropped from her elbow to the belt loop of her low-rider jeans. His hand felt warm against her body. She couldn't wait to get out of Legacy High and be anywhere else alone with Blake. They signed out of school and left in Blake's old car. "Where do you want to go? What do you want to do?" Blake asked as he laid his right hand on Nila's thigh. The warmth of his touch radiated throughout her entire body and made her shiver.

"You know, I really want to be alone with you in the woods. But I really think I need to speak with my mother once more before all hell breaks loose tonight. So do you care to take me into the clearing just behind my house?"

"Of course not. But don't you think your grandmother has you prepared?"

"Yes. She has taught me how to control my strength and my power—how to concentrate and bring my soul forward. I know that when Lorelei comes for me we have to bolt for the old tree at Legacy High. I just feel like a sitting duck—not knowing when to expect the fiery tendrils of hell to lap at my heels. I just need some reassurance from my mother."

"I totally understand. I would do anything you ask. You know that. So to the clearing behind your house."

Blake drove Nila straight to the farmhouse. Neither spoke a word, each lost in their own thoughts. Blake pulled into Nila's driveway and walked around to open her door. He reached down to her, and she slipped her hand into his. He gently pulled her up into his arms and hugged her, pulling her very soul into his like the moon pulling the tides. "Nila, above all, remember that I love you," he whispered into her ear, making her grow warm in that special place. His warm, sweet breath sent cold chills up and down her spine. Nila grew weak in the knees. She loved the feeling that she got when they were close like this, but at that time it was way too distracting. She had to see her mother.

"Blake, I love you. I will for the rest of this life and the ones to follow. I have to see my mother now. Then I can concentrate on us until Lorelei rears her ugly head." Nila kissed Blake with the slightest brush of her soft, delicate, sweet lips against his.

"I know. I just want every minute with you that I can steal." Blake dropped his arms, releasing his hold on Nila and stepping to one side. "Nila, call to me if you need anything."

"Thank you, Blake. I will." Nila began to walk, glancing over her shoulder at Blake, and then continued her journey into the thicket behind her house and on into the clearing.

The sun rays fell upon her shoulders, warming her through and through. Nila reveled in the feeling of the sun. She felt he presence of the raven. Since the protection spell, Nila felt him but more so when she was outside, especially in a peaceful place like the woods or the lake. Nila no sooner said the words than her mother appeared. "Momma, I need you once more before the battle with Lorelei. Please come to me."

Her mother was before her in an instant. "Oh, my darling Nila. You need not be frightened. I will stand by your side, the sisters will stand by your side, and Blake will stand by your side."

"I know. I just needed to see you once more to make sure I have done everything I was supposed to do. I didn't leave anything out, did I?"

"Nila, you have worked hard with your grandmother, you have inherent powers within you, you know how to connect with them, and you have raven. You need nothing else. Your grandmother did teach you that you don't need spells if you know how to be one with magic, right?" Mary laid her beautiful hands upon Nila's.

"Yes, ma'am." Nila squeezed her mother's hands.

"Then you are ready. Go now to Blake. He needs you, and you need him. Make sure to see your father before you have to confront Lorelei." Mary pulled Nila in close. She felt as though she were a child again. She felt so warm and comforted. She never wanted to leave her mother's arms.

"I will. I promise." Nila held her mother tight.

Mary knew that she needed an extra few minutes of comfort with her. Mary she must be patient with Nila to give her extra security for what she was about to face. "Nila," Mary spoke above Nila's head while still holding her, "you are strong, but I know that you need a few minutes with me to feel safe like you did as a child. You let me know when you are ready for me to leave. Okay?"

Somehow, that's all Nila needed to hear. Those few words from her mother gave her the inner strength that she did not know existed. She gave her mother one last squeeze and pulled away. "Thank you, Momma. I am ready to let you go. I have found my inner strength. I am ready to face Lorelei—whatever may happen. I love you, Momma. Go in peace. Blessed be."

Mary Jones smiled proudly at Nila. She kissed her on the forehead and faded away. "Blessed be, my darling Nila."

Amazingly, just as Nila's mother faded away into a mist, Blake emerged from beyond the thicket. Nila thought what a beautiful being he was. She likened him to an angel, her guardian angel. Blake smiled, and Nila knew that everything was right in the world. She smiled back and motioned him over. She just wanted to be with him—right then and right there.

Chapter 16

Nila lay naked in Blake's arm on a bed of thick pine needles in the clearing. "I really needed that closeness with you," Nila looked up into Blake's eyes. She felt lost in the blueness of them, like she was floating in the crystal blue lake.

Blake brushed Nila's black hair from her face. It was sticky and damp from love. He smiled down on her, "I needed the closeness, too. More than you know. All these years that I was not with you, I was not with anyone." Blake kissed her glistening forehead.

"I wanted to know. But I was also afraid to know. Afraid that maybe you had been with others. That's why I hadn't asked. I am so happy to know that it's only been me. Believe it or not, that makes me feel stronger—stronger as a person and stronger as a couple."

Blake kissed her in a way that made her feel like their souls were merging into one. His open mouth pulled her soul forward, and her open mouth allowed his to enter her. This kiss was deep and passionate. They had shared deep and passionate kisses before but not like this one. It was different. It was more than physical, it was spiritual as well. Nila could barely breathe as Blake's tongue intruded and his mouth covered hers. It was amazing the way that she could feel his essence becoming a part of her.

Then the unspeakable happened. Someone was there with them. Nila pushed Blake away.

"What is it?" Blake said, surprised and concerned.

"I heard something." Nila grabbed the clothes that were closest to her—her panties and Blake's shirt.

Blake pulled on his pants and slipped on his sneakers. Nila latched on to Blake's arm in fear. She still had pine needles sticking in her messy, damp hair. Blake couldn't help but take a minute to absorb the raw beauty that was only Nila. He stepped in front of his peasant priestess protectively. Nila held fast to her nobleman's arm. They were both shocked to see Dawn Gale Williams at the edge of the thicket. She stepped out and walked toward them.

Nila squeezed Blake's arm. "What is wrong with her? She looks like a mad woman."

"I don't know. What is she even doing here? This is your family's property." Blake stayed in front of Nila with his left arm slightly behind holding on to Nila.

"Well, well, well. I wondered where you two were off to. Why am I not surprised?

The closer Dawn got to Blake and Nila, they could tell something was not right. "Oh, my God." Blake held on to Nila tighter. "Get to the car. Now."

"What is it?" As the words fell from Nila's lips she realized what disturbed Blake. It was Dawn's body, but someone else was emerging. It was Lorelei!

Nila screamed, "I know. Run!" Nila gripped Blake's hand. They ran through the thicket, down through the back yard, and to the car. Nila ran fast and hard, paying no attention to the blood oozing from her bare feet—cut from sticks and sharp rocks. As they fled the clearing, they heard the terrible but familiar screams that belonged to Lorelei.

"I'm coming for you Nila Jones! I killed you once! I will kill you again. This time I will destroy you forever!"

Ice ran through Nila's veins. The two young lovers jumped into the car and fled toward Legacy High.

"David Jones! Come quick!" Ruth yelled out as she saw her granddaughter flee for her life. She knew exactly what was happening.

"Mother? What is it?" David questioned as he ran to the kitchen. He looked out the window in the direction his mother was looking. Before Ruth could answer they both saw Dawn. But it wasn't really Dawn. Someone else was in her.

"My God. We have to get to Legacy." David ran to get his car keys.

Ruth grabbed his arm. "David. You know how this must end. We cannot interfere. We have to stay here. If we go, we will only be a distraction for Nila. We could cause her death."

David fell into his mother's arms, knowing she was right. He wept like a child.

At this point, Dawn had transformed entirely into Lorelei. She stood in the front yard and yelled into the house at them, taunting them. She knew, too, that they would be a weakness to Nila. She also knew that the house was protected and that she could not harm them. There was an invisible boundary that Nila and her grandmother had put into place a few days earlier. They had cast a protection spell with the help of Mary and the raven.

"This house is protected. We are protected from your evil!" Ruth yelled out the window.

"I know you are protected, but she is not. No matter, I don't need you. You're weak and of no consequence to me." Lorelei turned and ran in the direction of Legacy High.

Ruth and David knew that it would all be finished in a matter of a few hours. Little did Lorelei know that Ruth and David were very strong in their ability to protect Nila—that was to just sit and wait. That took all the strength that they could muster.

Nila's heart sank as she realized she failed to keep her promise to her mother. She was not able to speak to her father before she confronted Lorelei. "Mother, forgive me," she whispered as she clutched her Celtic knot. It was the same pendent that her father had given her as a child. It was a family heirloom. She felt close to him when she held it. Nila had held it a lot right after her mother had died when she was away from her father and felt vulnerable. A wave of warmth flowed through her body; it was her mother's spirit.

"It's okay, Nila," her mother whispered into her ear.

"Tell Daddy I will be fine. Tell him I love him," Nila whispered.

She heard her mother respond, "I will. You be strong. Don't worry about your father." Nila felt her mother's presence leave.

Blake and Nila continued to speed toward Legacy, not saying a word to one another. Both were thinking about what was about to take place. Wondering if they could survive this time around.

David and Ruth sat on the couch in silence, holding hands. Mary appeared to them both in the flesh as she had so many times to Nila.

"Oh, Mary." Ruth said in a shaky tear-filled voice.

Mary walked to the mother and son and knelt at their feet. "Don't be fearful. You have taught her well. She will be fine. She will be home soon, and there will be no more concerns of Lorelei."

Mary turned to David, "My darling, David. Nila is upset because she didn't get the chance to speak to you before she left. She wanted me to tell you that she was sorry for that and that she loves you. She wants you to know that all will be well. It will end as it should. I will be there to protect our daughter. I will keep her safe." Mary hugged David and kissed him with the kiss of a young lover. David couldn't help but weep. With that, Mary faded away.

"She has to go to Nila. We have to be patient and wait." Ruth hugged her son as if he were once again a child. And so they waited.

Nila and Blake reached Legacy High. They bolted from the car, Nila still barefoot and bleeding. With joined hands, they ran toward to the massive old tree with Lorelei close behind.

"Oh, girl, you can run, but it will do you no good. Your fate is sealed. It is in my hands!" Lorelei laughed an ungodly laugh that sent chills run through Nila.

Nila almost stopped. She slowed slightly. Blake pulled at her. "What are you doing? Come on. Don't listen to her. Run!"

Finally they were in front of that tree. Nila's muse. Nila's tree of life.

"So are you ready to face your destiny? Are you ready to die?" The witch laughed as the wind whipped around her.

Nila was surprised to see the weather change drastically. She knew that the witch was strong, but she didn't realize until that point just how powerful she was. She controlled the weather. Lorelei held out her hands, drawing down nature—calling the wind, the rain, and the lightning. The boughs of the old tree bowed and creaked at the whims of the witch.

Nila and Blake held hands so tightly that Nila knew that no one could separate them. She knew that Blake would never leave her side. Nila had to bide her time. She couldn't move too fast. She had to draw Lorelei closer to the tree. That shouldn't be too difficult, after all, Lorelei wanted Nila dead. Nila knew that all too well. Nila and Blake backed up closer to the tree, leaning up against the trunk. Nila felt the familiar sting of the bark scratching against the flesh of her bare legs and bare feet. Blake and Nila stood fast and clung tightly to one another.

"Remember, Nila, don't let fear come forward. Trample it down and hold it at the bottom of your soul. I have always loved you, and I always will. I will not let go of you as long as there is breath in my body." Blake kissed Nila on the cheek.

"Oh, how sweet young love is. But it is no match for me. You're no match for me," the witch screamed so loudly that Nila knew surely her voice would break the windows of the school. The witch moved in closer to Nila. "It's almost time isn't it? Time for your powers to come to you. But I will do as before and destroy you before you can accept." Lorelei moved closer and closer, floating above the ground. Her clothing billowed in the wind. Her hair whipped wildly at her face. Lightning raged around her, and rain beat down all around. She called down hailstones. Then Lorelei was right in Nila's face, grinding her teeth and reaching out to take hold of Nila—to take the very life from her.

"No, witch, young love is not enough to protect us. But old love is," Nila spat at the witch.

"What is this feeble talk?" Lorelei questioned in agitation.

Nila squeezed Blake's hand, letting him know she was about to make her move—that the time was now. "Mr. Raven, come to me know. Protect me!" Nila screamed as loud as she could above the thunder, the lightning, rain, and hailstones beating down around them.

"What? What's this?" Lorelei yelled out in confusion. She chanted her spell to bind Nila's powers.

Nila felt nothing. The raven was protecting her.

The witch finished chanting. "Now you cannot accept your powers. I have bound you from the ones you had and the ones that you were to receive. This time I will not let you get away. I will destroy you here and now." The witch reached out her hands and began to chant again.

Nila let go of Blake and instinctively outstretched both arms. She called out to her mother for protection and for the sisters and other ancestors to gift her with what was rightfully hers. "Mother come to me, I need your protection. Sisters, all ancestors of the Jones family, come to me and gift me with my birthright."

The witch stopped her chanting and screeched out in a horrible voice, "What are you trying to do? No one can help you, and there will be no birthright!"

The clouds parted. There were rays of beautiful pink, yellow, and blue lights shining down on Nila. Nila's body lifted into the air high above the tree. One by one, each of the Jones' ancestors bestowed each of their powers upon Nila.

Blake knew that Nila was to be granted her birthright, but he had no idea it would be like this. Each time a power was bestowed upon Nila, she writhed in pain. Blake wanted to help but could not. He cried out to her, but Nila could not hear.

The witch stood in horror realizing what was happening. She feverishly chanted her destruction spell. But nothing happened. Nila was protected. "How can this be!" she screamed. "No! You are bound! You cannot accept this! You should be dead!"

After all the ancestors had delivered their powers unto Nila, the sisters blessed Nila with their powers and finally Mary Jones came to Nila and granted the power that she had possessed when she was alive—the power of the raven. Once the last power had entered Nila's body, Blake was amazed to see huge black wings sprout from his young lover's body. They were the wings of a raven.

Nila flapped the wings and stayed in the air. Nila couldn't believe the way that she felt. Above all, she felt the power of the raven consume her entire being.

Blake stared at Nila, thinking how beautiful she was, even with and especially with those shiny ebony wings of a bird protruding from her delicate body. He felt consumed by her exquisite uniqueness.

Nila was no longer protected by the raven, she no longer needed it. She had received her birthright. Now she had to face Lorelei—witch to witch. Nila knew that it would not be easy because Lorelei was outraged. Lorelei shot beams of electricity from her hands toward Nila.

Angered Lorelei yelled, "This cannot be! How can this be so? I bound you!"

Nila instinctively held her hands in front of her to block the attack. Blake stood there helpless. He was her protector, but he had no way to turn the tide. He didn't know what he could possibly do. He did the only thing that he could think of. Blake charged Lorelei.

"Blake! No!" Nila called out in fear.

Lorelei simply flipped her hand as if she was swatting at a fly and sent Blake sailing through the air. He landed against the tree and lay at its base unconscious.

Anger rose up within Nila. She bombarded the witch with blasts of fire from her hands. The two witches pummeled each other relentlessly, neither gaining nor losing to the other. It was an even match. Suddenly, Nila saw something she could not believe. Mrs. Carver! She was headed toward them.

"Mrs. Carver, no! Get back!"

Mrs. Carver paid no attention to Nila. She ran to Blake and scooped him up. "Blake, Blake! Wake up! You have to save Nila. Only you have the power to tip the table."

Blake opened his eyes and saw a blurry Mrs. Carver. "Mrs. Carver, run. Get out of here! It's not safe!" He started to stand, and Mrs. Carver pulled something from under her long coat. Blake couldn't believe his eyes. It was his sword from a life long ago. It was the sword that had killed the soldier. He immediately knew what to do with it.

He took the sword from her and stabbed the ground with it in the exact spot that he had spilled the blood of the soldier.

Lorelei screamed out, "No!" She turned just in time to see the soldier rise from the base of the tree. The soldier turned to Blake for only a second and smiled. He then entered into Lorelei. This was enough to weaken her. She screamed in pain. Blake descended on her with the speed of lightning, plunging his sword deep within her chest. He withdrew it and staggered back.

Nila seized the opportunity to finish the witch off. With her giant night wings flapping, she came down upon Lorelei and picked her up. She carried her high into the ebony sky. She held Lorelei with one hand and placed the other upon her forehead. "I now cast you out of the body of this girl. I now cast you into the pits of hell, into the abyss where you will never be freed, where you can never again harm anyone."

A black cloud of smoke left the body that Nila was holding high above the tree. The misty black cloud descended into the ground at Blake's feet. As he looked back at Nila and the body she was holding, he could tell that it was once again Dawn Gale Williams. His heart sank knowing that he had plunged a sword deep within her chest. He had killed her. He was devastated.

Mrs. Carver watched on knowing all along that Nila was capable this time of defeating Lorelei. Nila had to defeat Lorelei in order to avenge Mrs. Carver's soul from a life before. A life as a chambermaid that had been taken by the hands of Lorelei for helping a young nobleman to escape her clutches.

Nila knew what she had to do. She knew what she had the power to do. What the right thing to do was. Nila scooped the empty shell of Dawn up close in her arms and put her lips on Dawn's lips. From below it looked like a kiss. It was. It was a kiss of life. Nila breathed life back into Dawn's limp body. She laid her hand on Dawn's chest, and the deep wound from the sword closed, leaving no trace of having been there.

Dawn looked at Nila, knowing exactly what had happened. She remembered everything. Dawn was literally born again. She wrapped both arms around Nila's neck and held her tightly. "Oh, Nila, I am so sorry for everything. Please forgive me. Can you forgive me?"

Nila whispered into her ear, wings still beating, holding them both high in the air. "I forgive you, Dawn. All is forgiven."

"Thank you, Nila. Thank you for everything."

Nila came down slowly to the ground, gently releasing Dawn who fell instantly into Mrs. Carver's arms. "Oh, Mrs. Carver."

"It's okay. You need not say a word. Here, sit."

"Ursula. Is it really you?" Nila begged.

Blake was astounded, "What? How could you remember?"

Mrs. Carver shared, "I have always known. I had waited on you, Nila, for many years. Lorelei killed Ursula, or me, in my past life for helping Blake escape. The same wizard who helped you, Blake, also helped me. He gave me the gift of memory. I retained everything from my past life and knowledge of how to help in this life."

"How did you come by my sword? Lorelei had it when I escaped," Blake asked.

"I stole it from her in hopes of returning it to you some day. It remained in my family as an heirloom all these years." Mrs. Carver helped Dawn up, and they walked back toward the school.

Blake and Nila fell into each other's arms. "Is the soldier free?" Nila asked.

"Yes? All is as it should be."

"We should go and let Daddy and Grandma know everything is okay and that it's all over."

Blake reached up to touch Nila's wings. They were as soft and smooth as silk. He gently touched them, caressing them with such tenderness and love that it filled Nila with ecstasy. She was a little embarrassed that she had forgotten about having them and having left them exposed.

"So, will these beauties always be exposed to tease me?' Blake smiled.

"No." Nila bumped him with one of her majestic black wings. "They retract at will." She began to pull her wings in. In a matter of seconds they were hidden beneath the soft flesh of her back.

Blake slipped his finger into the holes of his torn shirt that Nila was wearing. He cautiously ran his fingers across the flesh of Nila's back where her wondrous wings had been only seconds before. There were no signs that they had been there. He was amazed once again by Nila.

"Let's go back to the farmhouse." Blake put his arm around Nila and guided his beautiful peasant priestess to the car. He admired her beauty under all the bruises, cuts, and scratches. He couldn't wait to lay down with her and hold her, knowing that they could sleep in peace; that they would never need to worry about Lorelei again.

Nila stared at her young nobleman all the way back to the farmhouse, knowing that he had been the one to save her, knowing that their love had saved each other, and knowing that they were free to finally be together with no fear. She loved her handsome nobleman deeply. She reveled in her feelings for him.

They arrived at the farmhouse where her grandmother and father were waiting on the front porch swing. They stood and greeted the young lovers. They went into the house together—Nila and Blake to tell the story and Ruth and David Jones to hear the story.

The End

Coming Soon

The Choice

www.ingramcontent.com/pod-product-compliance
Lightning Source LLC
Chambersburg PA
CBHW060142130626
46556CB00006B/2454